SOUL
STORIES

ZENAIDA CUBBINZ

ISBN: 978-1-910370-37-7 (Stergiou Limited-Assigned)
ISBN: 978-1-503256-99-6 (CreateSpace-Assigned)

———————

Copyright

Soul Stories
Copyright © Zenaida Cubbinz, 2014
Cover Image: © Ankdesign | Dreamstime.com

Print edition
ISBN: 978-1-910370-37-7 (Stergiou Limited-Assigned)
ISBN: 978-1-503256-99-6 (CreateSpace-Assigned)

eBook edition
ePub ISBN: 978-1-910370-39-1

Published by Stergiou Limited
Suite A, 6 Honduras Street
London EC1Y 0TH
United Kingdom
Web: www.stergioultd.com
email: publications@stergioultd.com

DEDICATION

Soul Stories for my heart and soul;
Suzannah Danielle & Geoffrey Adrian
and all those who make up the collage of my life

CONTENTS

AND THE YEARS CAME BETWEEN THEM   6

KAMARIA   20

THE HOURGLASS   46

SHAME AND SCANDAL IN THE FAMILY   65

THE CITY OF JOY   80

THE KEYS   93

THE CONFESSION   104

THE OLD HOUSE   114

PREFACE

Soul Stories; because they have soul; because they are real. Because they are a part of me, of who I am; because they reach out and softly touch someone's life; somehow, sometime, somewhere. The collection is inspired by the patchwork of people from all walks of life that fate has brought my way, with whom I have chanced to cross paths, who have until now dwelt somewhere in the deepest crevices of my mind. I have shaken them loose, dusted out the cobwebs, added colour and conjured up silent tongues that speak with words blotted over pages of white and black.

To all those wonderful people... I give you "Soul Stories."

AND THE YEARS CAME BETWEEN THEM

"And the years came between them" is a poignant tale of two very ordinary, middle class people who are years apart in age and their struggle to love and live the life they want. Set in so called modern India, in a town that hasn't changed over the last hundred and fifty years or so; a town where people still worry about society and what it dictates. This is a story of life's challenges and sacrifices where Indian society rules; a story that looks into the hearts and minds of its people.

"It would never work", they said. "What on earth would people say? How are we going to face people? You're too old! He's too young! or, "She's too old" and "you're too young ; you don't know what you're saying!" You two don't know what you're saying!" The sound of their heightened angry voices buzzed in my head. They did nothing to conceal the shock, the shame and the absolute disgust they felt. It throbbed and ached with ferocity like never before. Nothing made sense anymore, nothing mattered. Or did it? I really didn't know. It was over. He'd said those three fateful words just last night-"It's over Nicole." Part of me refused to believe it ever would be. But I knew somewhere down in that deep broken heart I'd have to live with the pain of losing him. And all because I was too old; and he was too young. Did that matter so much? What was age to us? It was just a number; a number that didn't matter at all when we were together. And that was why we fell in love in the first place; because it didn't matter right from the start. I was thirty two and he was only approaching his twenty second birthday.

The fact that there was ten years between us didn't bloody matter at all. Who cared? Certainly we didn't give a damn about the world and what it thought of us. We were in love, we were happy and damn, we were good together. I lacked the spirit of youth, the spirit that was so alive in him. He lacked experience in the ways of the world and the courage to venture out into the unknown. And then, unlike me he wasn't the type to throw caution to the winds, say to hell with the world and take chances. Unlike me, he wasn't a rebel. He was the boy next door. Handsome, charming, with an acute sense of humour he somehow always made me smile. But that wasn't all. I sensed in him a sense of responsibility and maturity beyond his years. I found in him understanding, affection, acceptance and love. I had finally found someone who wasn't intimidated by the fact that I was older, more experienced, more educated, had seen a bit more of the world than he had, could do and had done things that he hadn't dreamt of doing, was a single mother and had a four year old daughter. He revived in me the spirit of youth, the spirit that made me dare to do things, to take chances, to be silly at times, to laugh, to dress up and feel good about the way I looked and most of all to love. And I made him think about future and success, career, life, experiences and the desire to want more than what the present had to offer. We were one of the Ashton Kutcher's and the Demi Moores of Indian society; we belonged to the few of today who dared to be different not because that was what we set out to do or because we revelled in the gossip that was made over us or the fact that people hung out of their windows just to watch us together but simply because it so happened. And that in itself made our relationship so horrible and classified us as outlaws.

And yet there was this boyishness that is natural to any twenty one year old; a boyishness that I quite enjoyed and which kept me feeling younger. They assumed it would make me silly and frivolous and the laughing stock of society. I agreed to let them be the judge of that especially since I didn't really care. After all I was a rebel and then life had taught me that if you do good people talk about you simply because they haven't done what you have managed to achieve. If you do bad people still have a lot to say and if you do nothing at all people still find it in themselves to talk about you. I have learned to obliterate society and people from my list of priorities and to follow my own mind and heart. And here was a good man with a good unblemished heart; a man without guile and cunning who had not been tainted by the world and all its vices; a man that was willing to love and be loved in return. Did they think me foolhardy enough to give him up without a fight? And what of him? Did what he wanted not matter to them at all? Did the fact that he was happy not bring smiles to their faces? None of it mattered to them. That two people years apart in age could be so obviously in love with each other was scandalous! And the days of their own youth were conveniently forgotten when many of them had married more than once, some had enjoyed torrid affairs with total strangers or worse still, friends of their husbands, despite being married and staying married to keep up appearances. And what of those that had so recklessly eloped with partners out of their community and religious faith? All was conveniently forgotten. The slate was wiped clean and society prepared to sit in judgement over us.

We didn't matter. What we wanted was never even considered. And why would they anyway? They must go on dictating to others, or however would they manage to maintain their stronghold over the minds and hearts of people? How on earth would they dictate the precinct of what was acceptable and what was not if they didn't waggle their tongues in futile and endless gossip, spending hours on the porch of some old fogies home where they gathered to share and mutilate the information they had managed to collect mainly by word of mouth or by resorting to eves dropping on other peoples conversations. And the strangest part was that only that generation of older people seemed to care; only they seemed to want to live other people's lives for them. Only they foresaw our future together as bleak and filled with gloom. And of course they knew it all.

Sadly we found ourselves in a no win situation. And so we did what they wanted. What they expected us to do. We parted ways. The memory of those three words that he so reluctantly uttered, sitting there in the living room of my father's house will remain with me always though the tone in which he said them, the expression and the clarity of his voice might fade with time. But the essence of his words will remain with me for they hit me like a thunderbolt; took my breath away and left me speechless. I had underestimated the power of a woman and a mother. I had failed to comprehend the hold she has over her sons and her ability to emotionally blackmail them into doing what she wanted. I had failed to take into consideration the fact that Indian mothers live their children's lives for them for the most part. They tell them where to study, what to do, what to major in and what professions to take up, who to marry, what their wives should wear, where to sleep and how many children to have; not forgetting the fact that their grand children would bear names of their choosing and approval. So what chance of survival could I possibly hope to have against a seasoned mother of three sons and one extremely pretty looking daughter in whose opinion I was a cradle snatcher – out to get her poor innocent brother and lead him to the slaughter house; to ruin his life and his hope of any success and happiness in the future. Quite honestly, I wasn't the least bit intimidated by a bratty nineteen year old who thought her looks and colour and her foul language on her facebook wall would keep me at bay. I smiled for though I am usually the non interfering type, once in a while the woman and bitch in me does make herself obvious and I quite enjoy putting in place anybody who thinks they're too good for the rest of us.

Separation was new to him, more new to him than to me for being older and having seen more of life including one failed marriage that left me broken for a very long time, I knew exactly how painful it could be. Or I thought I knew. As for him, he was devastated; he tried to be brave and strong and to do what mama wanted, to stay away from 'that woman' as I later learned is how I was referred to. But it wasn't long before I was in tears on the phone and we were back to calling and texting each other on the quiet. In the subsequent weeks we had two more break up's that didn't last more than a week in each case.

And so began our secret affair, so to speak. Secret assignations followed in an assortment of places that included, laughably, the internet cafe, the park upon the hill with the little lake at its foot and the Chinese restaurant all of which were fraught with tension of who would see us and report back to our families. I for my part felt like a schoolgirl at having to resort to such means, means that were adopted by college kids. But I went along with it and more often than not I was the one who badgered him into meeting simply out of love for the boy who was so unlike others of his age; so uncomplicated, so untainted by the perverse thinking that has crept into the minds of young people these days. I loved the fact that my age simply didn't bother him; that he could lecture me with all sincerity and I was surprised that I took it all in good spirit mostly because most of it made perfect sense and also because I knew he genuinely cared. And when I needed to talk sense into him I had to do so carefully so as not to seem like I knew it all; not sound like his mother and not sound insulting and bossy like he once told me I did. I learned in the months that ensued, to weigh my words carefully with him though he never did bear grudges and was willing enough to forgive my unintentional bossing.

On the infrequent occasions that we did meet, we managed to enjoy our few stolen hours together. Time seemed to fly and it was always time to get back home even before we wanted it to be. We chatted laughed, talked of the future that seemed a blur at the time but we kept the fire of hope going and took courage in the fact that nothing lasts forever, not even the bad times. We had no assurances but each other, no comfort but each other and no support but each other. Nobody understood and nobody cared. But when it came time to waggle their tongues and hurtful and endless gossip, then strangely enough, everybody cared-a little too much if you ask me. Then there was old aunty from next door whose only mission in life was to speak ill of anybody and everybody but herself. She couldn't stand her daughters in law; from her talk of them that much was obvious. But then we can't really hold that against her for isn't it the mission of all Indian mothers in law to gossip and speak ill of their daughters in law with a vengeance that is totally admirable? And what about those women who have no other occupation that to wait upon their men- lords and masters of their homes; when they are done with their house work and when evening draws near they are seen chatting with each other from their tiny box like balconies or gathered in the living room of one household sipping chai and exchanging 'news' as they prefer to call it, or on the pretext of taking the children out to the park they could be seen gathered together deep in conversation, on their faces myriad expressions that changed from concentration, to surprise, to shock, to seeming pity and then back again for they soon found some other person to tear to shreds, and they would begin over again. These were women who thrived on gossip, women who varied in age, social status, culture, religion, language backgrounds but held together as if their life depended on it simply out of the urge to gossip. They poured out of their homes with one single purpose in mind – to tear to shreds the reputations of others of the same sex. Women who ranged from the young, newlywed next door just being initiated into the gossip game, the young mother of the little boy who cried too much, the mother of two teen aged girls in whose opinion her daughters were never capable of doing any wrong and when the girls were seen leaving the neighbourhood oozing oomph, dressed in clothes that would make a lot of heads turn, including those of the older married men, their mother would always find time to blame some old lecherous man for ogling at her girls. And then there were the middle aged lot - the older ones and the veterans who had been young so long ago and conveniently chose to blot out any memory of the scandalous events of their youth. The fact that some of them might have had extramarital affairs, eloped with sister's husbands, borne illegitimate children and enjoyed walking down the aisle more than once conveniently seemed but hazy images of someone else's past. The fact that their own families are composed of a motley of characters; children from various spouses or partners doesn't seem to be an issue. But they were ready to bear down upon us who dared to fall in love, us who dared to be different with unforeseen vengeance; so vehement was their attack that news of our so called relationship reached the farthest ends of the Earth probably at the speed of light and as I was chatting with a friend from Auckland, New Zealand on facebook he very indirectly broached the subject of my personal life.

And then there is the rare species of men who though are men, happen to be bestowed with the woman like quality of gossiping and taking immense pride in it. They are the lone wolves who go out of their way to hunt for information that they with great skill and dexterity twist out of shape and blow out of proportion when gleefully passing it on to the women whose gossip group they belong to. These men are indispensible to the women for they socialize with other males and manage to get out information regarding their whereabouts and comings and goings. And so, though the women may despise them for being the way they are the hypocrites in them do not allow them to keep them at bay for how else would their stream of constant gossip be kept going?

These men are the ones who have no scruples. They are those who will stoop to any level to get what they want and whose mouths are probably the biggest and inexhaustible part of them. They do not work sincerely and manage to keep their jobs by working hard at carrying tales and buttering their superiors, they seldom change jobs for fear of having to work hard to gain firm ground with the bosses all over again and are content to stay where they are as long as they manage to enjoy the favour of their employers. In return for supplying information on each of their colleagues, they have the privilege of doing almost no work and blaming others for anything and everything that goes wrong at the office. Such are the people that small town Indian society has to contend with; unfortunately for us, we were the victims this time.

And then there was my family to contend with – they at first adopted a don't care attitude but it wasn't long before it was evident that they did care - about what society would say and how ashamed they were going to be when people saw us together and found out that we were a couple. Support and understanding and a little bit of reasoning coupled with patience was what we expected. We couldn't have been more wrong.

Having made my point about small town Indian society and its drawbacks, it may be suitable to focus on the two people who caused tongues to wag in the first place; and to highlight just some of the problems they face. Secret assignations have an excitement of their own; the feeling of apprehension mingled with just a touch of fear and expectant anxiousness of whether they would make it out and back to their respective homes without being seen can be a challenge in itself. Here we were faced with exactly that challenge and somehow, that seemed to take the joy out of meeting in secret. To add to that was the big question of where do we meet or where do we go? Being the small town that it is I guess you could can we didn't have many options. And being the people that we are, we were choosy about a lot of things so our meetings were far apart and the few hours we managed to salvage were spent taking a long ride out of town and then another long ride back with a few minutes of standing by the river or sitting in a roadside restaurant sharing a drink or a snack and all the while wondering and praying that we wouldn't have a flat tyre and would make it back home in time. And during all that time we had to contend with the added fear of being seen together. If that happened the grapevine would work overtime to ensure that the entire community knew about it and definitely our families would be told with such relish and exaggerated panache that they would be in an uproar that would last for weeks with parents ranting and raving; I for my part would be secretly followed wherever I went for weeks to come; so much for being an adult and living my own life.

He would go home to what I call 'petticoat government' and hanging onto mama's apron as most Indian men do. I somehow keep being reminded of the book 'Sons and Lovers' every time I think of Indian men and their mothers who seem to own them. I have seen my own mother mollycoddle my brother, two years my junior to the extent that it has seemed disgusting and I have often wondered how a man can allow himself to be so dependent on his mother and to be treated that way. I have been called 'cold' on occasion when I have erroneously voiced my opinion on the topic. And so to petticoat government he would return and there he would stay firmly rooted until the pangs of loneliness began gnawing at our insides and we felt the urge to go through the motions of another secret assignation.

Such was our so called relationship. I remember one occasion in particular when the summer heat was getting to us and we happened to be in the city where we stopped rather reluctantly at a roadside vendor for a glass of sugarcane juice.

I also remember him giving me strict instructions to keep my face covered for fear of being seen and hurriedly gulping down the juice; I drank so fast that I hardly tasted it. We were gone in less than five minutes. Such was the nature of our infrequent meetings; fraught with tension and apprehension. Whatever little joy there was was overshadowed by darker things. And we weren't the type who revelled in the adventure and mystery and the thrill of taking chances. We felt cheated; why couldn't we just be like people in a relationship in any other more liberal setting should be? We felt we were right; the setting and the people around us were all wrong. And we couldn't change that try as we may.

Life is never complete without choices. Some say, "when God closes one door He opens a window." And some believe in the hand of fate, the element of luck, Karma or Kismet as I had so often heard it referred to by my Arab friends. I chose to believe in the hand of God. In the fact that He acknowledged our efforts in trying to do things right and seeking our parents approval at the very onset. I for one decided I had to get out which proved easier than I thought it would be. I soon found a job with a law firm in south East Asia and prepared to leave. I was gone in less than two months; so much for Indian society and its rules. I smiled at the thought of getting out of there. Now all I had to do was wait until the time for him to follow; and if his love was true as I believed it was, I knew he would. I was wrong once again. Indian society emerged the winner. I lost him to his mother and the scores of Indian mothers who would have supported her. I could almost see her, gloating over her victory at keeping her son. I was a loser she kept saying.

Love knows no boundaries, accepts no rules and follows no one. Indian society might control how we live; it might decide what is acceptable and what is not, it might control the body and mind of a person but the heart is a free spirit. It wanders where it wishes at will, feels what it wants and loves and hates as & when and who it pleases. It cannot be bound by chains. It is the essence of every human being and it makes us who we truly are. It is the one thing that cannot live without, cannot be separated from even though we may spend the rest of our lives physically apart. And when our heart lies within that of someone else it is but inevitable that the two should be united until death. The years ahead looked bleak, but there is always the element of hope.

The birthing

One hot and seemingly endless summer night, like all other nights, the heat seemed to be worse than ever; it seemed to rise up out of the earth and fill the empty spaces with consuming ferocity. Dalila lay in a sweating heap upon a mat on the floor of the family's tent. She had been lying this way for quite a while and had lost track of time. The minutes seemed like hours and the hours seemed to be endless. She was a strong woman but the child within her seemed reluctant to make its appearance in the world. Dalila had been lying in the hope that the child she carried would leave her womb; she bore the pain with clenched teeth and let out only the most occasional groan. She tried to keep it quiet lest her husband Rashid and the others hear her. The old midwife bent over her and with a look, encouraged her to push harder. She pressed her hands on Dalila's stomach and massaged in circular motion. Dalila uttered a silent prayer and almost before she finished, her prayer blended with the makings of a deep throated moan as her child left the warmth and safety of her mother's womb and was delivered. The old midwife, Dalila's aunt smiled her toothless twisted smile and caught the infant as she slipped from within her mother's body and into the world.

KAMARIA

Kamaria was thought of as a child who would bring the family luck. She had eyes that shone and seemed to light up at the slightest provocation. Kamaria was beautiful like her name which meant 'like the moon'. Her skin was dark as night like soft velvet and her close cropped curls somehow made her more beautiful. She was the epitome of her mother - beautiful to look upon and beautiful to the touch. There was much rejoicing the night of her birth. She had been born on the night of the full moon; it was definitely a good sign. Her father Rashid had slain a goat to feed the family and proudly held up his new daughter for all to see. The other families huddled around and marveled at the new infant who would suddenly invade their lives and would be the preferred member of the family. They were in awe of the child for none of them had been born on the night of the full moon. All feasted and eyed Rashid as he smilingly played host to the well wishers that came to share in the joy and the faint sadness at the lack of a son in Rashid's eyes was lost upon them all.

The moon child, as she came to be called, was the third daughter that Dalila had given birth to. Young though she was, she seemed spirited and demanded attention. With the passing of days Kamaria, the little moon child grew and as she lay upon a woven palm mat upon the earthen floor of the makeshift home that Rashid had put together to protect mother and child from the force of nature's elements, she took in the world around her. Her world consisted of the smells and sounds of the home; the voices of her siblings, of nature's creatures, the smell of freshly baked bread and maize. The occasional smell of fresh blood and meat as Rashid slaughtered an animal behind the home for a feast. But most of all her world revolved around the sound of her mother's voice and touch. Dalila would sing to her songs of old; of ancient warriors, of great chiefs, of mountains and trees and magical animals that existed in the recesses of her imagination. She would hear the soft patter of her mother's feet as she moved around the shelter of the home preparing food for her family and going about her daily chores. Kamaria took in all the sounds and turned her little head towards them.

When she was hungry the moon child would let take it upon herself to cry with vigor and announce to all those within the vicinity of the home that she needed feeding. Dalila would leave her work unfinished and in haste, take her into her arms and place her at her breast. She would then sing to her child as she suckled. The sound of her voice was like velvet and had a deep throaty ring to it. It soothed the hungry child almost immediately and she fed in contentment. She was soon asleep. The shelter would be quiet again and Dalila was free to return to the care and interests of the rest of her family.

The days passed and the seasons changed. Kamaria left her palm mat upon the floor and ventured forth to explore the world around her. She walked later than the other children and Dalila was worried. Though she encouraged the child to walk, held her by the hand and guided her forward Kamaria seemed hesitant and afraid. She would turn to face her mother and bury her face in the folds of her dress. Two summers after she was born Kamaria was still walking into things and falling over. The ability to walk without falling eluded her. Some of the younger children were amused at her inability but her mother was distressed over it. One night as she sat with her husband Rashid over dinner, after the rest of the children were asleep she broached the subject of the child's walking. Rashid laughed and said she was slow; there was no need for worry. Then he looked at the beautiful woman that sat beside him, extinguished the oil lamp that lightened the room, took her in his arms and lost himself in her warmth.

Dalila had been happy when her moon child was born. Rashid, her husband had not felt the same. He had wanted a son, who would grow up to be brave and strong. A son, who would marry, and from whose loins in turn would come more sons. But she was a beautiful child and so he hid his displeasure. When Kamaria began to walk Dalila's fear had been realized; they soon discovered, much to their disappointment, that Kamaria was blind. She walked into walls, fell over things that lay in her path and found it difficult to even put food into her mouth without first feeding it to her nose or ears. Dalila had been sad. As she lay on a sleeping mat upon the floor each night she cried silent tears for her child. She took special care of her daughter with the sparkle in her eyes that didn't see.

The after years

The days passed slowly, as they do in the mountains, where life is hard and monotonous. Dalila absorbed herself in her daily business of taking care of the family and Rashid, the provider did his best to ensure that their bellies were full and that they were safe from the beasts that hovered near during the cold cruel nights. Winter came and with it, the promise of a new child that grew inside Dalila's womb. She would have to prepare for the birth in the cold harsh winter. But she was happy, and she counted the days until the baby would come. Rashid was happy and hopeful too. This time Inshallah he would be blessed with a son. But it wasn't to be. And Rashid was disappointed once again.

With four daughters and no sons, Rashid was ashamed to face his people. He resented the pitiful glances thrown his way when he went out in public. He envied Jamal, his neighbor with five strong young lads, all the fruit of his loins as Jamal often boasted. When the men gathered for the communal prayer and breaking of the fast during the holy month of Ramadan it saddened Rashid that he went to it alone. It saddened him that he ate with the old men, and shared the meat and rice and bread that they had laid out before them. During his quiet moments when he bent his forehead to the ground in prayer, Rashid sighed and whispered, 'Ya Allah!' as one who is weary of life. He lacked courage to question the will of the Almighty; he knew it was not his place to do so. But deep down within him he longed for a child and at the commencement of the early fajr prayer, after he had washed himself in the trough that lay filled outside the shelter, Rashid whispered, 'Bismillah-e-rehmaan-e-rahim.' May the will of the Almighty be done.

Dalila sensed her husband's disappointment and a deep sadness came over her. She wept for her time of sorrow had begun. Her worth as a wife had diminished in the eyes of her husband and she feared that she would soon be cast aside, for hadn't Allah given man the right to marry four wives? Wives who would bear him sons? Rashid's interest in his wife had taken on a different turn. He no longer looked at her with the light of love in his eye. He didn't watch her as she bent over the cooking pot, humming to herself, with a half smile on his face. When she washed, he didn't stop to brush the stray lock of black curly hair that had escaped from beneath her hijab and fell languidly about the side of her face. And when he came to her at nights, only on some nights, his lovemaking was quick and harsh; barely lovemaking at all and he thrust into her with a vengeance; merely satisfying his carnal need.

The blessing

Dalila's belly grew with the passing of days and the child within her was soon ready to come. She waited patiently for the day when she would renounce the weight that she had carried for almost nine months. Young and strong though she was, the constant child bearing ever since she had married Rashid fourteen years ago, coupled with the hard life in the mountains had taken its toll in her and her body had weakened steadily with every child she bore. On the night her son was born, Dalila sat at the fire baking fresh naan and singing as she worked. Before her lay a plate of meat, skewered and cooked to perfection, the succulent taste of which was her husband's favorite. The song she sung was a love song, a song that she had sung even before Rashid had ever laid eyes upon her. She had been young then; only eleven. The naans cooked, and Dalila heaved her heavy body up; every muscle in her reluctant to bear the weight of her unborn child, and walked with deliberation, into the shelter. A sudden sharp bout of pain cut into her and all at once she feared for the child that lay within her. Eyes wide in horror, she called for help and the eldest child came running up to her. She sent for the midwife who arrived breathless and ready for a birth.

When Dalila lay in a mass of sweat with the child in her refusing to leave its mother's womb, yet eager to enter this world Rashid had been worried. He had sat by her bedside, a pile of goatskins on the floor in the shelter. He had held her hand and whispered sweet nothing's to her and at some point of time his lips moved in prayer. He had prayed for a son. And he wanted this child to be born. As he looked at her swollen belly he wished it would all be over. He longed for the child to come forth. He longed for a son. The midwife sweated over her and massaged frantically at the bulge in her but the child was unyielding. It went on all day and long into the night. Her groans of pain grew more frequent until the child in her finally slipped out and with it she breathed a sigh of relief. In the early morn just before the moon disappeared, Dalila gave birth to a stillborn son. Rashid held up the baby and his disappointment manifest itself in a guttural moan. The child lay still and covered with blood on a goatskin rug upon the floor. Rashid steeled himself, folded the right half of the rug over the left and carried his son out into the waxing grey of morning to lay him to rest.

Dalila was even more grieved than Rashid. She prayed and wept and begged Allah for a son. In the years to come she gave birth to two more daughters. Rashid distanced himself from his wife with these subsequent births and Dalila's desolation and realization and belief that she was not one of the blessed ones; that she would not bear male children for her husband was strengthened. The lack of male children made them the talk amongst the small clan of mountain dwellers. Delila was looked upon with pity by the older women and with scorn by the young single lasses who flaunted their youth, their virginity and their ability to capture the hearts of the men in the clan. When she walked down to the watering hole, where the women gathered to replenish the water of the clay jars and the goat skin bags, and to exchange some little bit of gossip they might have picked up on; where the young lasses dressed in their best, with their hair tucked seemingly under their hijab's, but always managing to somehow set free a stray lock that lustfully fell across their face and never failed to attract the attention of any man who set eyes upon them giggled and hopped from rock to rock and engaged themselves in noisy laughter, only to be silenced with a stern look and verbal admonishment from the older women. All this frivolity and gossip coupled with the looks of pity, both angered and saddened Dalila. She secretly loathed the beauty and youth of these young lasses and forgot her days of youth when she had been one of them. She began to stay more and more within the confines of the shelter and would feign physical sickness, and an excuse to send her oldest, Zenya out to fetch water, feed the animals, and do other household chores. In truth, Dalila was sick at heart and sought repose from her useless life. She prayed fervently to Allah, the merciful, the giver of all things but was half inclined to believe that she had knowingly or unknowingly angered the great one and had lost favor in his eyes. And then there was Rashid, her husband, the man who came to her when the children were asleep, and thrust into her, not because he took pleasure in the act but more out of a desire to prove himself to his fellow men by procuring, through his act of copulation with her, a son.

Her youngest son, the seventh child, was born on Friday, the holy day. The male child that she carried came forth into the world healthy and wailing. Rashid, overjoyed at the birth of his son, fell to his knees and with outstretched hands gave thanks to the great and merciful Allah for his bounteous blessing. He seemed to care not that the woman he had married, the woman who had come to him no more than a child, the woman who had given him her body, to do as he pleased and had borne him six other children, all of them beautiful had suffered in doing so and that childbirth had taken its toll on her body. He seemed not to care that Dalila now lay dead before him upon the pile of goatskins on the floor. The dark blood that flowed from her insides spilled silently over and soaked into the animal skins. Dalila's death he looked upon as the will of Allah, the almighty and merciful; the giver of life and death; Allah; the all seeing one; the one who knows best and must not be questioned. That evening, before dusk, Dalila's body was wrapped in a white shroud and she was laid to rest with the briefest of prayers, in a grave that Rashid, along with the young sons of some of the men had dug beneath a large flat rock that overhung it further up the mountain.

The void

With Dalila gone, the children seemed to be afraid. And though Rashid spoke kindly to them they seemed to fear him. When he instructed them to do something, they did it but not because they wanted to or enjoyed it. They did it because they were afraid. Suddenly the family seemed to be at a loss. The children felt it more than Rashid did. He seemed to be the same; cold and unaffected by the death of Dalila. Since Zenya was the eldest, it fell upon her to take care of the home and the family. She inadvertently took on the role of 'mother' to the younger children. Rahid showed no sense of relief at this nor did he express any kind of feeling at not having to trouble himself with the everyday upbringing of his children.

To Rashid, the fact that he had lost a wife and the fact that he had a daughter who was blind seemed a sign of weakness on his part. It irked him that he would never find a husband for the girl and he would have to take it upon himself the take care of her. It also irked him that he would get no dowry if she weren't to marry.

Kamaria missed her mother Dalila who was gentle and kind. Kamaria remembered the way her mother's hands felt when she touched her. She remembered the sound of her voice as she sang the children to sleep and told them tales of animals and great warriors. The moon child smiled as she thought about her mother, and then her eyes filled with tears as, for what was probably the millionth time, she wondered what her mother had looked like. Kamaria had never been blessed enough to see her. When Juma, the seventh was born on a cold wintery day, Dalila had taken one last look at the girl child who stood beside her, whose fingers clasped her hand and she cried for her moon child whose big brown eyes held no light. Then she closed her eyes, whispered a prayer and died.

When fate confirmed that Kamaria lacked sight Rashid reacted by distancing himself from her. Rashid was disappointed and he showed it. He stopped playing with Kamaria, was often angry with her and as she grew older, he spoke less to her. When she heard the sound of his sandaled feet approach the shelter she would call to him in her own childish way and attempt to run to him. She failed to see the displeasure that was evident in his look or she might have stayed where she was and no sound might have left her lips.

Kamaria was the only daughter who didn't work in the field. All her brothers and sisters even Zenya, the eldest who took on the role of mother and caretaker of the family, worked in the field with their father. They lived on the little money they earned from selling potatoes, maize and beans in the local market.

Kamaria spent most of her day at the cooking fire, milking the cow and helping Zenya by doing what she could for her brothers and sisters. She had learned her way around the shelter and as long as things were placed where she was used to them being, she was able to navigate with apparent ease. She had learned to follow sound, and smell and was able to chase the sheep up along the path and out into their pen to lock them away for the night.

Life without her mother was hard for the little girl. Her older sister took care of her wants and needs. But the void that the death of her mother had left grew deeper and wider with the passing of time. Zenya was there to see that she was fed, clothed and to dry the tears she cried when she wasn't too busy with her house work. But Zenya wasn't her mother; her mother with the soft velvet voice, who sang songs and told her stories. Her mother who taught her the Holy Quran and that Allah was the all seeing, all powerful merciful God. And Zenya didn't smell of freshly baked naan and sour yogurt, mixed with the sweeter scent of crushed rose petals. Kamaria missed it all and grew more withdrawn with the passing days. But the void that the death of her mother had left grew deeper and wider with the passing of time. She had grown more withdrawn with the passing days. She spoke only when spoken to and whenever possible answered with a nod or simply by accomplishing a task that was assigned to her. The younger children humored themselves, cruel though it was, with the thought that besides being blind their sister lacked a tongue. Kamaria listened to all their taunting without a word. She would wait for night to come; as she lay upon her mat she would call to her mother and give vent to her tears. Sometimes she would be angry at Dalila for leaving her. Then she would ask why she had not cared enough to take her moon child along with her? She would, in childish tones, chide her mother for wandering off and leaving her moon child to her own devices. And then she would weep and beg her mother to forgive her for being a bad child and for all the trouble she had given her. Her tears wet the mat and seeped into the earth until the never ending blackness of her world was encompassed by the night and she fell asleep.

Black, white and gray

Her world comprised of black, white and grey. The morning sun, when she turned her eyes towards it seemed to shine radiant and white. She would squint at it for unusually long periods of time without batting an eyelid – a feat not so easily accomplished by the other children who were blessed with sight.

The rest of the time Kamaria's world was black – as the darkest night. She wondered what the sky was like; her sisters told her it was blue…she wondered what 'blue' was. She loved the sound of water but no amount of describing could form in her mind a picture of the liquid beauty of it.

And then there was grey…her days seemed to pass in a blur

of grey. Dull uninteresting days they were. Nothing much happened to her. She worked in the shelter, she pottered around the tiny living space, picking up after the other children, occasionally tripping over some abandoned object that had, at some point of time occupied their fancy. She went from living space to cooking space and huddled over the fire as the smell of fresh baked naan gradually wafted into the air and filled it. When she was done with her chores she would go outside and sit in the sunshine. She would dare to lock eyes with the great orb and stare it in the eye. She never had to blink and look away. Her life was black, white and grey…each had its own part and one never seemed to encroach upon the territory of another.

Deep in the recesses of her mind, Kamaria had grown accustomed to her three colored world where even the most simple and vivid things were but a figment of her imagination. But she resented it. She wished she could see; she wanted to gaze upon the moon for she had heard so much about it – since she was born upon a night when the moon shone in all its glory and splendor. She wanted to see the water, to look upon the blue sky and know what it meant to gaze up at the stars on a starry night. She wanted to open her eyes each morning and meet the day. She wanted to challenge the sun, to stare at it only to admit defeat and look away as the other children had to.

Kamaria lived her hazy existence. She knew no more and had no opportunity to hope for better. Rashid was distant and often intolerant of her inability to see and continued to express it in whichever way that happened to catch his fancy. At times he took pleasure in watching her stumble and fall over some inanimate, trivial object that he chose to place in her path. When he was consumed with the spirit, as she thought of his drunken bouts, Kamaria would hide herself in the corner of the shelter by the cooking pots and no amount of Zenya's coaxing could get her out. But consumed as he would be, Rashid would find her, order her out and take it upon himself to torment her. His laughter would remain with her throughout the night and long after. Her only weapon against his tormenting and the laughter of her younger siblings were the hot tears that flowed silently each night as she lay huddled in her threadbare dress that had obviously seen better days under a goatskin rug upon the floor of the shelter. That was her time, to let the tears flow and to talk to her mother. A time which was hers alone, unwatched by leering eyes that allowed her to pour out her heart to Dalila. And she silently prayed to Allah that her mother, wherever she was, was listening.

Rashid

Of late he had taken to bringing his friends into the shelter late at night, when all the children were tucked away in bed and engaging with them, in discussions of all sorts; from politics to trivial gossip and even the details of their many triumphs with the women they managed to find on their travels into the towns. They would laugh and describe in vivid detail their escapades with these women. These were men who prided themselves on their prowess, their ability to capture the attention of any woman they chose to, and they discussed at length varied subjects for they claimed men who didn't take it upon themselves to educate themselves and their sons in the ways of the world and its happenings weren't really men at all. The child Kamaria didn't fully comprehend these discussions at first but they remained with her while she grew. Zenya always stayed close by her side on nights like these and she was thankful for the warmth and comfort of her sister's body as they lay huddled upon the sleeping mat.

One night was especially eventful. Rashid had been home earlier than usual from the tiny vegetable patch that the family owned and maintained in order to sustain themselves. He brought with him aubergines and radishes and six rabbits that he set about skinning almost immediately. When he had done this, he went to the water trough outside the shelter and proceeded to wash himself vigorously after which he combed out his hair and beard and perfumed himself with the oil of attar – another rarity in the mountains where they lived. He seemed unusually lively that evening and the children were all sent to bed earlier than usual. When it was quiet, Rashid sat down outside the shelter and waited. The minutes ticked by and finally, the sound of horses being led up the far side of the mountain behind the shelter came to Kamaria's ears. She woke but remained as if asleep under the goat skin rug, unmoving and silent – making conscious effort to still even her breathing, for by some basic instinct she knew it had grown faster, and in her mind, louder. The horseshoes clicked against the hard rock and from the sound of it Kamaria gathered they were tethered out back, where the shed that held the goats stood. Her father wasn't a wealthy man and owned no horses except one rather old horse that he rode and that carried the bags of flour and sugar up from the town. The beast was old and slow but Rashid couldn't afford to have better.

The sound of the horse shoes stopped and was replaced by the soft thud of boots on the ground. Voices followed, deep throated gruff voices but somewhere in the melee of it all Kamaria was almost certain she heard the feminine rustle of fabric upon the floor accompanied by the faint tinkling of a bell. The voices retreated to the far end of the shelter, that part which had become Rashid's sanctuary on nights like these when he reveled in the company of the men who came to visit him.

However, tonight would be different. The gruff voices grew fainter within minutes and were soon replaced with the sound of horseshoes upon the rocky floor fading into the night. All that remained was the silence and the faint rustle of silk upon the floor and the tinkling bell - and the smell of a woman. A woman that was perfumed and bathed unlike any that Kamaria had ever known but had heard the older girls' gossip of. A woman they believed to be wanton and wayward and ready to please a man in the most unimaginable way.

From where she lay, Kamaria had no view of the goings on between her father and the woman and since she was blind Rashid went to no great lengths to ensure he and the woman were concealed from view. The other children lay in a huddle in another part of the shelter and a curtain; goat skins sewn together, separated where they lay asleep from Rashid and his female companion. Unlike when in the company of his male friends, Rashid spoke very little and when he did it was in hushed tones. The woman's talk was equally subdued but their conversation was suddenly interrupted with the distinct rustle of fabric being ripped and a deep throated groan that escaped from the lips of the woman. This was followed by heavy breathing that grew rhythmically faster and louder and eventually ended in short moans from both Rashid and the woman. The culmination came when she half screamed and Rashid uttered a long guttural moan. There was silence once again.

Kamaria was afraid. She failed to understand what had happened and was almost on the verge of waking the other children when she felt Zenya's protective hand upon her shoulder. Zenya hushed her and told her to sleep. The sounds of the night were quite alien to her. She couldn't remember a time when her mother had ever uttered such sounds and the thought of another woman in such close proximity to Rashid disturbed her. Something told her it wasn't quite right. She lay huddled under the goatskin rug unable to sleep long after the sounds had stopped. She listened for the sound of morning, for the first twitter of the birds, the cock crowing and the warmth that the sunrise brought with it. The smell of fresh bread in the oven is what usually woke the children and it was up to Kamaria to set about this task. Finally, she crawled out from beneath the warmth of her bed to begin the day's work. Hunger got the better of her and she concentrated on getting the bread in the oven. For now the woman and the events of the night before were forgotten.

The outsider

The muffled sounds of the night grew more frequent with the passing of days. Zeenya, now almost a woman herself, old enough to be married and sought after by the young and older men alike for her beauty seemed to understand the happenings of the night. She seemed to Kamaria, to share some hidden camaraderie with Rashid and on nights when Rashid came home consumed with spirit, humming a tune and went out to wash and perfume himself, Zenya took it upon herself to ensure that the children were fed and in bed before darkness fell. When all was silent and they lay upon their goatskin rugs in the far end of the shelter which had, over the years expanded and had come to be not just one large room, but a number of rooms, sleeping quarters for the girls, a communal living space where the family ate, a play area where the children sat around Zenya and listened to songs and stories and separate prayer areas for the children and for Rashid.

From where they lay, with the younger girls asleep Zenya and Kamaria lay in the darkness and listened to the sounds of the night encroach upon them. From out of the night came the sounds of lurking predators, the wolves and the hyenas that ventured abroad at night, the hoot of an owl and the scuttling of both predator and prey in the undergrowth. And at some point of time, in the melee of sounds her ears trained to make up for her lack of sight, and to pick up on even the faintest of sounds, would hear approaching horses hooves upon the rocky path at the rear of the shelter, the faint tinkling of bells accompanied by the soft rustle of fabric upon the floor, and soft sandaled feet that entered her father's private sleeping quarters and suddenly her nose was awakened into action and took in the strong, sweet smell of feminine perfume. What followed next was always a mystery to Kamaria, but in the silence and in the darkness she would often hear Zenya whisper, 'Ya Allah!' amidst the muffled sounds of fabric, deep and quick breathing, jerky body movements, strained but hushed groans, all of which would stop as suddenly as they had begun. Then the creatures of the night would occupy her thoughts until she drifted into sleep…sleep that was more often filled with dreams of her mother calling to her, laughing, singing and then suddenly walking away from her into the darkness. Kamaria would awake weeping and calling to her mother. Zenya was always there to put a protective arm around her and hush her back to sleep.

The grey of morning took over from night and the sound of birds awakened Kamaria. She rose, reluctantly and woke the other children by her side. Today was another day and she must get the fire going to prepare fresh naan for her father and the others before they left for work in the small field they tended. When she had the father going, Fajr, the youngest of the girls called to let her know that their father wished to see them all. She wondered at this rather unusual request and hastily took the naan out of the oven and left.

When she entered the communal living area Kamaria sensed the tense silence and the presence of an outsider. The faint smell of perfume lingering in the air told her all she needed to know. Rashid, his voice thick and gruff announced that Sameera was his new wife. The children were told to treat her with respect and generally not to disturb her. The woman didn't speak at all and when each child in turn was made to say, 'Sabbah-al-kheir' she uttered no words, but acknowledged them with the briefest nod of her head. When it was Kamaria's turn to greet her new mother, Rashid awkwardly announced that she was the child who tended the shelter because she was blind and couldn't be sent out to work in the field.

Sameera kept mostly out of the children's way. From the chattering of the other girls and Zenya's careful conversation she learned that Sameera was young, not much older than Zenya herself but was woman enough to know the wants and needs of men and keep them satisfied. It was not until much later, that she realized how useful such knowledge could be.

Sameera

She was born in a small village outside the city of Cairo, on the banks of the river Nile. Her mother, of whom she had no memory whatsoever had been a harem girl and by some unfortunate means had chanced to fall in love with one of her patrons, a man of high repute and had allowed him liberties that had led to her being with child. She had hoped that the man who professed to love her in return would whisk her away to a faraway land and marry her but it wasn't to be. Sameera was born in the harem, placed in a basket lined with soft linen and handed to an old lady who stood waiting at the gate. Money, tied in a drawstring bag was also handed to the old woman. That night her mother's body was removed from the room she occupied and prepared for burial at sunrise.

The first few years of Sameera's life passed in the company of the old woman who was neither cruel to her nor did she make any attempt to develop any kind of bond or affinity with the child. She bathed her, fed her and took care of her needs. She taught Sameera how to brush her long black silken hair and to make it shine like dark velvet. When Sameera was ten and even more beautiful than her mother she was taken to the harem and given a room of her own and a feather mattress to sleep on. She was given the company of two older girls who, though they lacked her beauty, had other skills that they had instructed her in.

Having spent her early life in the service of the men who chose to have her; being continually at their mercy for them to do as they would with her, to satisfy their carnal greed Sameera soon lost track of everything including the passing of time. When Rashid's visits to her grew more frequent and he proved more gentle than the others, for he was infatuated by her beauty and nubile prowess and finally when one day he proposed to buy her out for a price, for the first time in her life Sameera wept with joy.

Comaradrie

When Sameera came to live with them the atmosphere in the shelter changed. She was not much older than Zenya and was secretly glad at the prospect of having female company even though not much was said between them. The girl wife was however bright enough to realize her position as mistress of the household and wasted no time in establishing her position amongst the women of the home. The men and boys she knew from experience she would have no trouble with. They would readily accept her superior status without question. Juma was too young to cause her much trouble and failed to understand the fact that she had taken the place of his mother. He had no memory of his dead mother whatsoever and Zenya was the closest to having a mother that he had ever got. Kamaria, for lack of sight proved no problem; she kept mainly out of Sameera's way and for her, life went on as before. Zenya proved to be a tough nut to crack. She was reluctant to give up charge of the shelter and her position as head in the absence of her father. She walked around with a sullen look and a tight upper lip and was curt with anyone who chose not to obey her. Juma and the other younger girls seemed unaffected by her change in demeanour but Kamaria felt the mounting tension and was troubled by it.

One morning Kamaria was awakened by Zenya before time

for the fajr prayer. It was dark still and Zenya placed a hand over Kamaria's mouth and signalled to her to be quiet. She need'nt have done so for Kamaria sensed that something was wrong, terribly wrong and her ability to remain silent, save the rhythmic sound of her breathing kicked into place. The thick dark silence was broken by the sound of sobbing and what sounded like the ripping of material, intermitted with something harsher and more sudden; the sound of leather upon skin. This was followed by the slamming of a door and horses hooves which faded in the distance. The sobbing continued at a heightened pitch and when through the darkness the sounds of, "Ya Allah! Ya Allah!" and a desperate call for help did Zenya, holding Kamaria firmly by the hand intercede.

Sameera lay in a bloodied state. Her back and chest had been whipped by Rashid. Kamaria set to work on her wounds washing them and applying a soothing salve to them while Zenya busied herself with getting a fire going to cook her some food. Sameera, they now noticed was lean and her body needed feeding. She laid her head in Kamaria's lap and wept until she slept.

Rashid did not return home the next day and the children, sensing somthing was wrong asked no questions. The girls huddled together and soothed the still sobbing Sameera until sleep took command of her and lead her into its realm of quiet darkness.

Changes

The beatings continued, worsened and became more frequent. The girls drawn closer by their common dread of the man of the house seemed to seek comfort in the fact that they had each other. When Rashid was in the mood for violence he took pleasure in lashing out at either or all of the girls in the house and they bore their lot in silent suffering and tears shed in the darkness as they huddled together. Sameera's suffering was greater for she was subjected to his sexual advances and made to satisfy his need. She would wake up sore and bruised form within and when she squatted in the darkness to let the fluid flow from her she winced with the burning pain in her. Zenya and Kamaria made up for his ill treatment of her by feeding her well and soothing her when he had satisfied himself beating her.

One particular dark and cold night when the wind was howling in the trees and refused to grant them any respite at all the girls sat huddled in their sleeping area unspeaking; as though they dreaded the occurring of some forbidding evil. The thin goatskin blankets offered little protection from the cold and they felt almost numb with the cold. Rashid called to Zenya to come to him and when she did he spent a long time looking at her. She stood before him with her hands by her sides limp and her head bowed. He ordered her to wash herself and get dressed. Zenya tensed for she knew what that meant – she had never been faced with an order like this before. Tears stung at the corners of her eyes but she was a proud girl and she refused to give him the pleasure of seeing her true feelings.

The man that Rashid had chosen for Zenya was fifty years of age and had three other wives. His eldest son was older than Zenya and would have been a more suitable match for her. When she looked at him she knew that he wanted her in a way that was not at all sisterly for she was a beautiful young woman and would arouse the desires of any man who set eyes upon her. But she pushed aside the thought almost immediately for it was sinful to want the son of your husband. The nikah was over and she was gone forever. Kamaria and Sameera bid her a tearful farewell while Rashid watched expressionless.

That night Kamaria lay alone in the dark; Rashid, intoxicated from the celebration sent for Sameera and her screams of pain aroused in him an almost insatiable sexual need. When the morning came, and Kamaria went to wake her Sameera lay unmoving, cold and stiff. The blood had congealed around her and though Kamaria saw nothing of it, she felt the cold, thickness of it and knew that it was over.

Her guttural screams brought Rashid running and still intoxicated from the celebrations of the night before he stood before the limp body of the girl that had been wife to him and laughed. Kamaria could take it no more. In the cooking area, beside the oven where she baked naan each morning she thrust the knife into her breast and held it there. The blood flowed silently as if in mourning for the loss of her innocent life. She had, without seeing seen enough; and she could bear it no more. Life was only grey. There was no black or white. To her it was grey. And she wanted none of its dreary greyness. It had taken away all that she loved – her mother, her eyes, her sister Zenya her chance at life and a future, and Sameera.

All that remained was grey...and the crimson drops that flowed into the earth.

THE HOURGLASS

This is the story of two women; of the bond that exists between them. It's a story of love, winning, losing, dejection, struggle and life.

Tick -tock tick -tock

Goes the clock

Time waits for no one

It seems to say

Oh time please I beg you

Grant me but another day

She lowered herself onto the dresser seat, turned on the light and looked in the mirror. She was neither shocked, nor afraid, nor repulsed by what she saw; she was angered instead. She felt cheated by time the wretched one that steals the life out of one's eyes. And as she looked at herself the hot, salt tasting tears began to flow. The creature that stared back at her from the mirror was a stranger. A stranger that seemed wasted and worn out; an empty shell of a woman that was once filled with the zest for living, a woman that had once laughed and cried, sang and danced; a woman that had been so alive; a woman that was once her. But that was so long ago and the memory of happier times had all but faded and gone. Now all that remained was the face that stared back at her from the mirror. All that remained was the wasted away frame and that was her!

Cassandra sat there and let the tears flow. They felt hot against her sullen sunken cheeks and the tiny rivulets they made along the crevices of her skin were strangely soothing. She made no attempt to dry her tears and her hands lay limp upon her lap. The wrinkled face, not just with age but with loss of health that she saw each time she mustered up the courage to look in the looking glass disappointed her and brought on the tears and the regret once again.

The was tempted to draw open the curtains and let the sunlight in but sunlight was synonymous with life and happiness and the thought that she would never enjoy either pained her too much. She put aside the thought, willed herself to pick up the hairbrush and brush what was left of her hair. Every brushing left her scalp more visible than before – the effects of her medical treatment the doctors said. Cassandra hated chemotherapy and the sterile perfectness of the hospital rooms. She hated being there. She had hoped she would get used to it with time but she never did. It only made her resent it more. The clock struck one. It was time. Danni and Ross would arrive any minute now. She walked over to the closet, selected an orange shirt and beige skirt to wear and dressed herself, all the while refusing to take notice and dwell on the fact that her clothes hung on her skeletal frame. She covered her head in a pretty floral silk scarf – a present from Ross. It always made him happy to see her wear it.

She busied herself with setting places at the table. When the two young people arrived they greeted her with hugs that were warm and filled with love and made up for all the pain she felt. They brought with them a bottle of wine which she placed in the refrigerator to chill. It would do nicely during the meal.

Lunch was an enjoyable affair that lasted well into the early evening. She was always happy to have the children over for that was how she referred to her twenty three year old Danni and her twenty seven year old fiancée Ross. They had met a year ago when Danni was on holiday with friends in Greece. Ross was an architect who had fallen in love with the dark haired tall demure young lady the moment he had seen her. And when he heard her sing – he had made up his mind that she would be his wife and he had moved there to be with her. The couple had dated for nine months before moving in together. Cassandra was both relieved and happy for her little girl. All she wished for was to see them married. She could now prepare for her end which seemed to be drawing rapidly nearer.

Danni had majored in music and was a teacher at the local school. Ross and she had moved into their new home that they had chosen only a few weeks before and though the young people were loathe to see her live alone she was happy to see Danni with Ross, a wonderfully sensitive and warm hearted man.

As she watched them drive away she thought of the time when she had been a young girl herself – and had been so in love. Unfortunately for her, life hadn't been that easy, and she had ended up bringing up Danni alone.

Sam and she had married when they were both twenty three

and she was just out of university. Sam was a student of theology and they had known each other since high school; they had met in church when he was altar boy. Tall, lean and soft spoken, Sam had been so different then. He had pursued her and she had turned him down at first. When she was into her first year of post graduate school Sam had joined her literature class and things had taken a different turn. They were married soon after she graduated. He went to do a degree in religious studies and she moved to be with him.

The wedding was more than a simple affair. They had no money and couldn't afford more. Cassie had left the school she taught at early that day and taken the bus to the registrar's office. Sam was waiting for her there. It was over in ten minutes. Then they had gone for a bus ride all over town and had bought Chinese takeaway and eaten it in the park. After that he walked her home to the rented room she shared with another girl.

It wasn't until the next term began that Sam was able to take her to their own living quarters on campus where he attended class. It was in pretty bad shape, the walls needed plastering, the windows had no panes and the furniture was old and worn. But they were happy; it was home to them. They did their best to make it look and feel like home and settled into the routine of being husband and wife. Cassie had worked hard to provide for them while Sam studied theology. They had decided they wanted time with each other before starting a baby but six months after they moved in together into their home she discovered she was pregnant. Cass had gone to visit her mother and brother one weekend and had not been able to stop eating. She had been perpetually hungry and her brother had eventually gone out and bought her the home pregnancy test to take. The next morning confirmed Cass was pregnant. She was ecstatic. Sam had been in a state of shock. He hadn't wanted a baby until he graduated. A visit to the doctor revealed Cassie was twenty two and a half weeks pregnant; too late to have the abortion that Sam wanted her to have. And an abortion that she wanted nothing to do with. Cass was a mother; she thought of her baby as hers already and was mentally preparing for the day when she would be born. She just knew it would be a girl. Sam said it would be a boy. But she knew in her heart he was wrong.

Suzannah Danielle arrived on the 13th December at precisely 11:27am in the general ward of the Assembly of God Mission of Mercy Hospital. Sam was not there when she was born; he had a commitment – a Christmas gathering at the College before the end of term. He arrived later to gaze with awe at the tiny little girl that was his daughter. But he was too afraid to hold her.

Cassie went home three days after she delivered her baby girl by caesarean section to a pile of laundry that needed washing. On the eighth day she had her stitches removed. She went back to work when her daughter was twenty days old.

When Danni was little she was the tiniest baby that Cassie had ever seen. She was, at first afraid that something was wrong but was assured by the doctors that she was just small but would grow. By age three months they were proven right and Danni was like any other three month old.

And then it hit her. Sam told her he wanted out of the marriage, he couldn't deal with taking care of a baby; he had to focus he said on his career as a pastor. In the months after Danni's birth Sam had grown increasingly indifferent to Cassie and the little one and spent most of his free time out with his male friends. He got home when both mother and child were long in bed and asleep. Finding someone to care for Danni when she was away at school and teaching was her main worry but when a neighbour with a two year old little boy volunteered to take Danni over from her she was more than grateful. When Sam said he wanted her out she had nowhere to go. It changed everything. Cassie couldn't go back home to her father after she had walked out much against his wishes to marry Sam. So she took what seemed like the best option at the time; she went on holiday to visit cousins back in her hometown and spent a month with them. They loved Danni – all of them and went out of their way to lavish her with love and attention. Seeing her baby so loved and secure, Cass decided to go job hunting so she could move to live and work there with Danni.

One afternoon Cass' aunt called to her and informed her that her father was on the phone and wanted to speak to her. Though reluctant to speak to him, she was coerced into talking to him and was surprised when he asked her to lunch the following weekend. She accepted and when she and her baby arrived, Cass was even more surprised when her father asked her what her plans were. She told him she had plans to move back. When he asked about her marriage she told him it was over and that she was definitely not going back to Sam since it was quite obvious he didn't want her or Danni. It was then that her father invited her to move back home and she did.

And that had been the end of her marriage. Sam had asked for a divorce not long after and she had gladly given it to him. It symbolized the breaking of all unhappy ties for her. She had no desire to hang onto the unpleasant memories that surfaced every time she thought of him. It had also been the beginning of a lonely existence; an existence where she went through different phases, sometimes craving love and companionship, sometimes contemplating ending her miserable life, sometimes filled with desperation and hopelessness and yet at others she would be filled with drive and ambition and plans for the future. The loneliness and lack of companionship never left her. Cass missed having someone in her life. But strangely she didn't miss Sam.

Danni was a wonderful child and she grew into an even more wonderful young woman. She had inherited her father's height along with his good looks and thick black hair which hung down to her hips and swayed when she walked. Coupled with all of this was the fact that she was a demure young lady who carried herself with poise and grace. But the best part of her was her heart; she believed in the goodness of giving and was kind and gentle even as a child. And now she was woman; beautiful and strong yet gentle, kind and loving. Through her growing years the bond between mother and daughter had grown stronger and they had been not just parent and child but friends to each other. There had been times when Danni had exhibited extraordinary maturity and had mothered Cass; those where the times when Cass felt more blessed than ever to have her. When bouts of loneliness drove her to the brink of insanity Danni's love brought her back. When she had been given to tears Danni had patiently let her cry with her head in her lap and dried her tears. When she had to leave Danni with her father and go off to work Danni had understood and had told her to go and do what had to be done; she would be fine she said. Cass had marvelled at the strength of her seven year old. It had given her the strength to leave and go with renewed determination to work hard and save money for the pair to migrate to somewhere where they would have a better life.

Danni had been her strength all along. She wouldn't have made it without her little angel. Cass often wondered what she had ever done right to deserve a child like Danni. She was blessed. Cass remembered the time when a man she had dated had broken her heart. Danni had been there to help take away the pain; to tell her that there were better people in this world. She truly believed there were for at seven she hadn't really seen much of the world at all. Sometimes Cass felt like the child and thought of Danni as her little mother.

One day Danni had come home from school and announced that she wanted a father and that Cass should find someone to settle down with. She also wanted brothers and sisters she said. Everyone at school had them she said. She knew that she was missing out on something. It wasn't easy explaining to her that men didn't grow on trees and babies weren't delivered to one's doorstep by the stork. Eventually when she had seen her mother heartbroken after two successive relationships didn't last, Danni stopped asking for a father or brothers and sisters to play with. She seemed to have understood the fact that it was going to be just her mother and her. And that was all the family she would have.

Danni had seen her mother hurt and was wary of boys as a teenager. She didn't get into any of the high school relationships like most girls her age did. She kept things simple and kept the boys at bay. She knew some of the hurt they could cause and saw them as a threat to her happiness. Her friends nagged her about it and teased her for being so prim and proper but Danni wouldn't relent. She took it all in her stride. The boys in the locker room stopped discussing her when they found they weren't getting lucky or scoring with her. It wasn't until she had graduated from university and been persuaded to take a holiday in Greece where she met Ross that she had let down her guard a little.

Weeks before Danni had graduated from university Cass had been diagnosed with cancer. It came as a shock to both mother and daughter. What was worse was that it had spread to her lungs. Cass had woken one morning with a strangely heavy feeling. In the shower that day she had noticed a lump, the size of a large pea upon the underside of her left breast. She had later mentioned this to Danni and she had been adamant that her mother see a doctor. Danni had called the hospital to make an appointment for her. When Dr. Shelton saw had examined her she looked rather grim. What followed was an array of tests that left Cass both worried and drained. Danni was devastated at the prospect of losing her mother; a fact she did her best to hide for she knew that Cass needed all the strength she could get. The ensuing months were filled with trips to the doctor and medicines that needed taking. Cass lost her health partly due to the cancer and partly due to the fact that she knew she was a living time bomb that would explode one day and that would mark her end.

Tick-tock, tick-tock

Went the clock...

Cass hated the sound. It got on her nerves. Little things did. She hated the sound of water flowing and going to waste. She hated the wilting flowers on people's desks and coffee tables. She hated the scent of tuber roses for she said they seemed to remind her of funerals. She hated TV for it was either so full of violence or filled with images of happy people laughing, loving, and living life. In short she hated her life. It wasn't life to her at all. It was what she called existence. It was waiting upon death to arrive and being prepared for it to come just when one least expected or wanted it to; it was the knowledge that it would arrive when one was in the middle of one's happiest moments and steal it. She never really got used to the fact that her life was no longer hers anymore and that she couldn't live for Danni as she had been doing all these years. It belonged to death now and she saw death as the enemy. It drove her to fits of anger and resentment. Cass hated the sunlight. It seemed mocking to her. She shut herself up in her little home and ventured out only to get groceries. Danni hadn't wanted to move out and leave her mother but Cass didn't want her to be there when her end came she said. She had begged the girl to go and begged Ross to take her. It had been a tearful affair. Cass slipped further into her secluded world and was only happy when Danni and Ross visited. Then she shone and flitted about like a monarch butterfly with renewed energy after a good drink of wine. And when the couple had driven away she would go back into her world of seclusion and despair. Then she would tell herself that she was going to be mother of the bride and she couldn't afford to die before that; it always helped get her into living mode again.

When Danni had returned two weeks later looking happy and tanned she had told her mother all about her holiday and how the five girl friends she had gone with had been helped by Ross when they had lost their way one evening. Ross' name featured in all subsequent conversations. Cass had smiled every time Danni mentioned his name for she turned an embarrassing shade of red when she did. Finally she was able to get out from Danni the fact that Ross had taken her to dinner – just the two of them. And they had gone shopping together and visited the island of Santorini too.

Ross arrived a month later to visit Danni at their home. He was on a business trip he said but promised to spend a day with them. Cass had liked his easy, open demeanour and had seen that he genuinely cared for Danni and treated her with respect. The couple had kept in touch and six months later, Ross quit his job in Italy and moved to be with Danni. The couple had then moved into their own home but not after Ross had asked Cass for her daughter's hand in marriage. Cass had been shocked to know that men still did that- asked for the daughters hand in marriage. She thought it amazingly sweet. Ross explained that where he came from that was how things were done. Cass couldn't help but say yes. That night Ross took Danni out to dinner to a quiet restaurant where they dined and then for a walk on the beach. It was there that he showed her the ring he had chosen for her and asked her to allow him the honour of spending the rest of his life loving her as her husband. Danni had cried tears of joy and accepted. They were to be married before Christmas.

Summer changed to autumn and then winter. Cass watched the leaves turn from green to golden red and brown and fall. It made her sad to see them strewn upon the ground. That was the story of her life she thought. There was so much to be done, so much she would have liked to do but would never get the chance. She wanted so much to see Danni walk down the aisle and to give her away. She wanted to be the one there when her first grand child was born. She wanted to hold the little one in her arms and sing lullaby's and whisper sweet words in those tiny ears.

The day before the wedding Danni called to remind her mother that she would pick her up for her bridal shower. Cass thanked her daughter but told her that she wanted to save all her energy for the wedding. She was going to dance she said. Danni was immediately concerned and worried at her mother declining to be there. Cass assured her she was fine. When she put down the phone she allowed herself to relax and settled herself on the couch with a writing pad and a pen. She was in the mood to write.

On the morning or the wedding Danni was a bunch of nerves. She called and asked her mother to come over and help her get dressed. Cass was happy to have the last few hours with her little one. She picked up her keys and left a letter each addressed to Danni and Ross in its place. The moments that mother and daughter spent together were special. Danni would remember them for as long as she lived. Cass arrived to find Danni surrounded by a flowers, all sent from friends and well wishers. She set about putting them in vases and soon had the room looking like the garden of Eden as Danni said.

Cass washed and brushed Danni's long dark hair and begged her daughter to let the hair dresser get to work on it but Danni was adamant; she wanted her mother to do her hair and so Cass did her daughter's hair into a French knot and tucked into place tiny white flowers that made her look almost angelic. She trimmed and then painted Danni's nails in a faint pink and helped her dress. Then when her beautiful little girl stood before her looking radiant in her wedding gown, the body of which was adorned with tiny white seed pearls, Cass slipped off her finger a ring with thirteen tiny diamonds that she had saved for her little girl and promised her and handed it to Danni. There were tears in her daughter's eyes, for she knew it was the only thing of any material value that her mother possessed. Danni knew her mother had bought that when she worked in the middle-east and Danni was only four years old; she had bought it only because it had thirteen diamonds and thirteen had been the day Danni was born and because more than anything she wanted to be able to give Danni something of hers on her wedding day. To Danni it wasn't just a ring. It wasn't just thirteen tiny diamonds that were valued at probably fifteen hundred dollars. To her it was years of hard work, saving and sacrifice; it was a mother's love and the patient journey that she had made right until this day.

As she looked at her child's reflection in the mirror Cass was reminded of the day she had been granted her divorce and custody of her daughter. Sam's words rung clear in her ears and she had never forgiven him for what he had said. When the judge had asked why she wasn't demanding alimony Cass had said she wanted nothing but her little girl who was then aged four. She had demanded instead that Sam be granted no visiting rights and that he not see Danni at all, if he wasn't prepared to take on the responsibility of being a full time parent. He had readily agreed but he had a condition of his own; that Cass or Danni would at no point in the future ask him for any kind of monetary help – not ever at the time of her wedding, or lay claim to any of his personal assets at any time especially in the event of his death. The judge waived the six month waiting period and granted Cass the divorce in four days. And Cass had never forgiven Sam for what he had done to her little girl for the rest of her life.

At precisely three fifty five that afternoon Ross walked into the tiny church where they had chosen to be married. He had waited for this moment ever since he had set eyes on Danni that evening in Greece. He had vowed to love and cherish her even before he reached the altar. His bride arrived at exactly four o clock breaking the tradition of the bride arriving late; she was obviously too happy to be getting married to the man she loved to be late. Cass smiled at her daughters daring and thought of herself. It was something she would have loved to have done...if she had gotten married in a church with pretty flowers all around. But she was happy...more than happy that her little girl was getting the wedding of her dreams and she was grateful for the lease on life that she had enabling her to be there and witness this moment.

The sound of an organ playing penetrated her thoughts and she felt Danni's hand on her arm. "Mum, are you all right?" she asked. Cass smiled and answered, "Couldn't be better darling." Then she walked her daughter down the aisle to the wonderful man waiting there for her. She watched with tears of joy as they said their 'I do's' and exchanged the personalized vows that they had written for each other.

Liam Alexander and Keira Ashley were born on the second day of October the following year. Danni had been a happy mother to be throughout her pregnancy. Ross was over the moon when the babies arrived. He took to fatherhood with readiness and pleasure. Cass watched the family from the upstairs window of their home and smiled as husband and wife held their children and each other close.

The cold that year was awful. It chilled Cass to the bone. Late one night as she sipped hot chocolate from a mug that Ross and Cass had given her on Mother's day, Cass felt her time draw near. She walked over to the dresser where she had the letters addressed to Ross and Danni and placed them where they would be seen...just in case. But she smiled as she did so; she wasn't sorry to leave. She had come full circle after all. She had beaten death. She had been a daughter, a friend, a lover, a wife, a mother and a grandmother. Her life was complete and she had no complaints. And now her time had come. The sand in the hour glass had fallen through into the bottom. It was time. She was gone before first light.

Danni ripped open her letter with trembling hands. She hadn't stopped crying. Life was going to be so different without her mother. As she read the tears began to flow with renewed energy.

My Darling Angel,

I know that by the time you read this letter I will be gone...but please don't cry my angel and don't be sad for I am not. I am happy to have had so much time with you and even happier that I didn't have to share you with anyone all these years, selfish as that may sound. I am happy that God blessed me with you - and not just any other child; for you are and always have been special my angel. You have been my strength and joy...and I have lived a happy and complete life because I had you to share it with.

My darling I have regrets too...I regret all the tears you shed for me when I had to leave you with your grandfather and go off to work. I regret hot being there on your first day at school. I regret not being there when you learned to hold the pencil and not being able to teach you to write. I hated myself for teaching scores of kids and not being there to teach you my very own little angel. I regret that I wasn't there to pick you up and hold you close to me every time you fell and scraped your knee; or to dry the tears you cried when other children hurt you. But most of all I regret not being able to give you the kind of home and childhood that I believe every child deserves to have – a childhood filled with happiness and brothers and sisters and a father that you could look up to and call your own.

I know I have been far from perfect my love. I have not done the things and said the things that mothers do. But I have loved you in my own weird way...I have really loved you till the moment my eyes shut in death and the breath of life went out of me. I wish that I could have given you more...a better life, a better home, the things other children had and more. Sadly I had none of that to give. God for some reason desired that I must work hard for whatever little I did have and if I did that HE would bless you in turn. I hope I have done enough for you to get those blessings.

My darling, I know that you are truly wonderful, in every sense of the word. You have always had a golden heart; a heart that goes out to those less fortunate than you are, a heart that loves and gives and shares...you did all of this even when you were a little girl of five. When you were asked at school to collect all your old toys for the poor children, at the top of the pile was the new teddy and the little doll that you loved. That was so good on your part and made me love you even more...and be proud of you. I was always proud of you; the little failures you might have encountered along your journey from childhood into youth and then adulthood didn't matter to me for I knew you would be a winner in the long run; a winner at the game of life. My angel, it pained me to know that you were on stage in your school concert and that I wasn't there to cheer you on and hear you sing your little heart out. I would have given anything in this world to have been there all those times.

My darling I do hope you will forgive me for all my shortcomings and failures. I know I have failed you on many counts. But if there was ever one thing that kept me alive and gave me strength it was you. And I thank you for the wonderful life you have given me. If I didn't have you, the end of my marriage to the man who fathered you would have been the end of my life. I must confess my Angel, through the years when the two of us were together the thought of ending my life had crossed my mind. I was a coward to even think such thoughts and was ungrateful for I failed to see during those times, the blessing of you that I had in my life. I wasn't worthy of you my love but God was merciful and kept me alive, and happily alive I might add in your company.

I think also, of all the times in my life that you have mothered me. You have been the strong one, you have given me hope, you have been there to wipe away my tears and tell me it would be all right...and all when you were so little my darling. It is hard to think of you as my child sometimes... for you are so close to perfection; I see you as my very own angel from heaven. Almost like my little mother who takes care of me and watches out for me.

Thank you my darling angel; thank you for everything. I wish I could have given you more and that is my only regret. I grieve not that my life is over for I have seen it all. I have been blessed to watch you grow and find the man of your dreams and have the babies you always wanted. You have given me grandchildren and I have come full circle. I am not going to tell you to be a good wife and a good mother. I know that you will be nothing less than what God wants you to be. I am simply going to say goodbye my love, goodbye and thank you for a life so blest... thank you for being my little angel. I loved you till the end.

Your Mama

Cass

SHAME AND SCANDAL
IN THE FAMILY

A typical middle class Indian family, a town that hasn't changed in years, a working man, a housewife and their three teenagers.

He woke each morning at precisely 5:30am and after he had washed and dressed he proceeded along with his wife to the altar in the corner of the bedroom to say the morning prayers which he recited with such devotion that even the priests of the temple might be put to shame. The goddess Lakshmi would grant him blessings for his devotion and Anup Bhattacharjee was waiting for the day when he would be blessed. A slightly balding, short man with ample stomach, he appeared to have been blessed already and in reality, he had not much to complain about. Anup Bhattacharjee lived in a large old apartment building – in a flat upon the seventh floor. This was one of those apartment buildings that had been built during British times; it was large in size with ample space and a huge private terrace where hung a hammock that his children took pleasure in lazing about in. Mrs. Paromita Bhattacharjee looked even more wealthy than her husband, if size were anything to go by and she insisted on putting the red mark of Kumkum, the symbol of all married women right through the centre of her forehead, all the way back to the crown of her head. She wore her greying hair pulled back into a tight bun that rested on the nape of her neck. She was dressed, as all women of her community are in a traditional Bengali sari that was of the finest quality cotton. Bengali women never compromised when it came to their saris, they only wore the best Bengali cottons that money could buy- their husband's money of course.

Once her husband had seated himself out on the terrace and busied himself with the morning paper that had just arrived, Mrs. Bhattacharjee busied herself with brewing him his morning tea which she flavoured with elaichi. When she took the glass to him he merely grunted and went back to reading his paper. There was no need to rush today. It was Sunday, and he could take his time. Breakfast would be a heavy and late affair as Paromita, his wife and mother of his three children would take her time catering to the taste buds of her sons and daughter. He would have to take a back seat today.

In the street below the traffic got heavier as more people got up and about doing their Sunday shopping, visiting family and friends and generally getting about their business. The noise or the fact that a choir of crows had taken to singing just above his head didn't seem to bother him in the least. He continued his reading with seemingly genuine interest. Mr. Bhattacharjee liked the stock markets and so he turned to that section first, then he devoted his attention to the sports page and the very mention of Saurav Ganguly, brought a smile to his lips. He called to his wife over the din of the traffic and read out to her what the newspaper said about the Indian cricketer before immersing himself in the newspaper once again.

In one of the three bedrooms of the flat, twenty three year old Arijeet Bhattacharjee, an MBA in finance from one of the more prestigious institutions in the country, opened his eyes at the sound of his alarm. He sat up rubbed his eyes and headed for the bathroom. Once showered and dressed in his low rise jeans and Ed Hardy designer T-Shirt Ari, as he was called, presented him-self at the dining table. His mother, as if out of nowhere, appeared with a plate in her hand which she placed on the table before him. He was instructed to call his father for breakfast.

A little later, Kajol, his sister, who had just turned twenty one and was studying fashion, presented herself at the breakfast table dressed in a pair of skinny jeans that she wore low upon her hips teamed with a T shirt that looked like it was two sizes too small. And soon after her came the youngest Bhattacharjee, fifteen year old Debashish, who didn't bother with dressing or combing his hair at all. It was too much effort he thought; a total waste of time when all you had to do was run your fingers through it and it looked cool. His father didn't even give him a glance. He knew by now what to expect and Paromita Bhattacharjee thought it better to remain silent rather than enter into a debate over what was acceptable and what was not with her children. She knew she would stand no chance against the three of them.

At the breakfast table not much was said and the family

focused on the task at hand; eating with such gusto as only a Bengali can. When breakfast was done, Ari lounged around on the couch watching extreme sports and arguing with his girlfriend at the time, about where they would go that night. He wanted to hit Someplace Else but she thought it wasn't classy enough and suggested Moulin Rouge since all of her friends were going to be there.

Kajol ignored the stern looks of her mother and headed out with her boyfriend who lived a few blocks away. They were going to a movie she said, but her mother suspected it was more than just a movie and the thought of all that was possible besides the movie when it came to her daughter and her boyfriend Brendon, an Anglo-Indian boy that she thought very little of, sent shivers down her spine. Brendon didn't seem to mind at all that his girlfriend's mother wasn't happy that her daughter had picked, of all the nice young Bengali boys that she knew – friends sons of course, her daughter had lost her heart to this long haired lanky lad who smoked, drank alcohol and ate beef.

If her daughter's taste in men disappointed her she hadn't a clue as to how blessed she was that she hadn't met Ari's current girlfriend, a Spanish woman of twenty five who was on a six month holiday in India. She and Ari had run into each other at a disc and had gotten to dancing or grooving as they called it. They had both gotten drunk that night and had ended up in her hotel room. It was almost four am when Ari realized where he was and remembered the events of the night before. He had waited till the morning, called his best bud Sid and asked him to cover for him by saying he was with him all night asleep at Sid's place and then taken a taxi home but not before he had stopped at a Barista and ordered himself an Americano coffee which he downed in the taxi on the way home. When he got home his father and he had exchanged words and the parents didn't seem to have bought his story about being over at Sid's place.

And then there was Debashish; the youngest brat of the Bhattacharjee family. Debu as he was fondly called by his mother and sister, and mockingly called by Ari preferred to spend his time in front of his computer when he was at home and if not could be seen hanging out with friends at the maidaan playing cricket. He was his father's pet for in old Anup Bhattacharjee's opinion, Debu was the only one of his children with any drive or ambition at all. Debu said he would be the next Saurav Ganguly. That was left to be seen opined Ari and Kajol in unison. Debu didn't have a love life as such. The girl he liked at school preferred the more exciting fair, handsome Mark Williamson, an Anglo who was captain of the basketball team. Debu, short like his father, with glasses and no beard or body as yet knew he stood no chance with the girls as long as the likes of Mark Williamson walked the school grounds. And so he devoted his time to computer games and cricket. The geek preferred the company of geeks.

Anup and Paromita failed to penetrate the world of their children. Having grown up in a different time and being teenagers at the time both Mr. and Mrs. Bhattacharjee had come from modest backgrounds and had gone to school, studied hard and done well. Their parents could afford none of the distractions that their own children now enjoyed and so there hadn't been anything else to do but study. Paromita being a girl, had been subject to a lot of restrictions; none of the wear what you want and go where you want syndrome worked for her. Her mother chose all of her clothes-all traditional and before her sixteenth birthday she was a schoolgirl in saris. The word boyfriend was almost abusive in her home and she had married, without question the middle class Anup, four years her senior a bank clerk at the time with a more than decent income and a home in one of the nicer areas in the city. They had their first conversation the day they were engaged and it was then that Anup discovered that his wife to be had a passion for old Hollywood movies but had never seen one in her parent's home. The demure girl that he had married gradually changed into the traditionally bossy Bengali wife and Anup, as most Bengali husbands do, made no complaints; he seemed instead to take it as part of the ritual of being married. Paromita took control of the reins of the home and the bringing up of the children while Anup absorbed himself in getting promoted at the bank, reading the newspaper, following the sports news, changes in the stock market and keeping abreast of politics in the country.

And so when they were faced with three young people who were their children but belonged to a different world both husband and wife seemed inept at handling the situation. They simply didn't know what to say or do. They seemed unaware of the fact that their children had lives other than the ones they lived at home; the other side of their children seemed not to exist at all to them. The children never seemed to want their parents advice on anything and when Anup and Paromita had gone shopping for Debu's thirteenth birthday and had come home with a pair of brown trousers and a beige shirt for him to wear he had been almost insulted that they would expect him to wear something as monstrous as that and had gone into his room and locked himself there. He had emerged on the morning of his birthday dressed in unwashed jeans that hung low on his hips and advertised the brand of underwear he had chosen to wear as though he were the brand ambassador doing his job. They had been ashamed and were dreading the relatives coming to dinner that night only to find their children dressed in similar, if not more shocking fashion.

The parents failed to understand the aim of this entire generation of children. They seemed to take pleasure in looking weird, the bell bottom trousers, the drain pipes, the short little churidar kurti's, the long skirts they agreed were so much better. But agree as they might they could do nothing to change the way their children thought and dressed and acted. It was they said important to be part of the gang – to be accepted and so they went with the flow though both parents secretly thought it was more than that. They took pleasure in doing what the rest did and even greater pleasure in shocking their parents.

Ari left late that evening. He wouldn't be home before dawn he said. Something about spending the night with Sid he said. But his mother suspected that the Sid in question was one with breasts and a vagina; one that would lead her poor Ari astray.

Kajol and Brendon spent the afternoon out at one of the malls in town. The movie had turned out to be lukewarm and Brendon had been restless and irritable all afternoon. In the dark of the movie hall he had taken Kajol's hand and pressed it to his crotch. She had let him sweat, making no indication that she intended to give him anything. When the movie was done she had whispered, "Are your parents home?" Brendon smiled hailed a taxi and headed for his parents home.

Ari's Spanish lady love had won in the end and they had gone to the 'classier' Moulin Rouge where they had, as usual gotten drunk and after much dancing and drinking, ended up in her room and bed. When Ari arrived home next morning looking more than just a little hung over from excessive partying, as he put it his father sat him down and demanded an explanation. It was clear at the end of it all that nobody in the family bought his story. The fact that Ari was in love, or at least thought he was hadn't occurred to him until then and he suddenly knew what needed to be done. He was going to propose marriage and to hell with what his parents said. Yes, that's what he would do – just go ahead and marry the woman he loved and they would just have to accept it and live with it. Ari showered, changed and left for the work; his office was on the twenty second floor of a building and Ari worked along with two hundred others in the shipping division of the company that dealt primarily in the export of tea. It wasn't a bad position to be in for a twenty three year old fresh graduate. The pay wasn't bad either and Ari could afford to move out of his parent's home and into an apartment as he knew he would have to.

Two days later Ari had made up his mind. He couldn't stand going home to silence and 'we're so disappointed in you' looks from his parents. His siblings seemed to sense all was not right and kept their distance from everyone in general. It seemed like the entire family was doing a dance of avoiding each other. When he was with Eva he was happy. She sensed the change in him and wondered if there was something wrong. Ari was more gentle, loving and attuned to her wants and needs; he argued less and gave in to her more. When the weekend came, he however was adamant they skip the night at the disc and go somewhere more romantic and quiet. When they finally settled on dinner at a nice restaurant a little out of town Ari hailed a taxi and they drove there in silence. When dinner was done and they were walking in the lawn Ari thought it time to pop the question. The ring he had chosen was simply perfect he thought. The diamond would take her breath away. He felt the box in the pocket of his jeans. Eva walked beside him, their fingers entwined.

When she looked at the ring she was speechless. She stood there at a total loss for words; she just shook her head and looked at Ari. There were tears in her eyes. The look of confusion in Ari's eyes confounded her and she led him over to a bench, sat him down and told him she was sorry. She wasn't in love with him and couldn't marry him. She didn't want to get married she said. She wanted to travel and see the world, to experience all that life had to offer. She was too young to marry she said. And she was so sorry. They drove back in silence. Since Ari's home was first the taxi dropped him off and then took Eva to her lodgings. They never saw each other after that.

With Eva out of his life, Ari found he had a lot more time on his hands. He began to take an interest in his siblings and their lives. Debu was indifferent to his attention, but Kajol resented his intrusion until she figured out to her surprise that he was on her side. When their parents complained and grumbled and objected to Kajol's relationship with Brendon and threatened to find her a nice Bengali boy to marry, it was Ari who came to her rescue and defended the love birds with such ferocity that left her speechless and ready to hero worship her older brother. Ari had lost out in love and knew the pain of unrequited love; something his sister had never experienced and Ari couldn't bear the thought that she should ever have to go through the pain of it all. He knew Brendon wasn't the best for his sister, but he also knew that Kajol would be heartbroken if she lost him and knowing her as he did, she would turn cold and cynical; cynicism wasn't for her he thought, she was too young to turn her back on love and go through life believing true love was only a thing of the movies and story books and didn't happen in real life. And so Ari decided he was going to be on her side. He would talk to Brendon; he made mental note of that.

Now that it was established that the family was divided on the matter of relationships and suitable partners Paromita

Bhattacharjee moped around the house with a hurt expression that often gave way to tears in the presence of her children, especially when she knew they were watching her while her husband seemed to bury himself in his newspaper and the stock market news. Debu, as usual seemed indifferent but was aware of the battle of wills that prevailed in the home, and secretly wondered who would eventually back down and give in.

Twenty four old Brendon Grey worked for an advertising agency. Long haired, fair and handsome, he looked more the model himself. He had met Kajol at a party and had been immediately taken by her petite frame and her practical outlook to life. They had been discussing relationships and if what she said was anything to go by, he figured he had just met the most practical woman on the planet. Kajol had no qualms about letting people know what she wanted out of life. She was a strong, determined, focused girl with a great sense of humour and a laugh that turned him on. In the weeks that followed they seemed to bump into each other at social events; his friends sister's birthday party, a colleague's girlfriends home, at the disc he frequented on weekends and it wasn't until six months later that he had asked her out.

Brendon had never felt the need to look at another woman since. Kajol, to him was the one. But he wondered about her willingness to commit. She was only twenty; would she be ready to settle down to being a wife and raising children? Would she even consider him as a partner? Would she blend in and keep up with his Anglo upbringing and lifestyle? And would she be shocked by the fact that his family had no expectations from daughters in law other than to keep their sons happy? He had no answers. Only time would tell. Brendon thought about bringing up the subject of marriage, but then thought better of it. He would have to wait till she was ready.

On Saturday morning, Kajol left early to meet friends at the club for a swim and then to spend the day with girlfriends from school. She wouldn't be back until later that night she said. When she hadn't called or returned by 11pm her mother began to panic. Ari who was out playing pool with the guys from work took his mother's frantic call, calmed her down and said she was probably with Brendon. He promised to find her.

Brendon was visiting his aunt and cousins. He had been trying to call Kajol all day but her phone was switched off. In the middle of a family gathering that he had wanted Kajol to go with him to, he wasn't too happy and in no mood to talk to people but when Ari's number flashed on the screen his first thought was Kajol, and that she was in some kind of trouble. Ari was to the point. Kajol had left home at 7:30am and they hadn't heard from her since. Her phone seemed to be switched off. If Ari believed Brendon's story of not having heard from his sister all day, his voice gave no indication of it at all. He suggested they meet at the Barista near the Bhattacharjee home in fifteen minutes. Brendon said he would be there. When the cab he was in drove up Brendon was already waiting, his bike parked on the pavement. It was time to have a chat with Brendon and get some answers.

At 2:00am after two beers and calls to numerous of Kajol's friends revealed nothing, Ari headed home to wait out the rest of the day until he could officially lodge a police complaint stating that his sister was missing. He was however convinced that Brendon was as lost as he was and had nothing at all to do with Kajol's disappearance.

The door was opened by Debu who looked rather scared. On the couch sat his mother, in tears holding a letter. His father stood at the telephone and seemed deep in conversation. When Ari walked into the room he went straight to his mother who handed him the letter.

Ari sat in silence. He had been so wrong about Kajol. He felt like a perfect stranger. He had thought Brendon would be the one. Damn it! He even liked Brendon. Couldn't she have just gone and done what everyone thought he would do? Couldn't she have thought about what this would do to their parents? Hadn't he made sacrifices too? Why did she have to be the spoiled brat and ruin it all? Why did she have to do this? Why Arif? He was the guy from the store across the road. God knows how much education he had. Ari suspected not very much; he had been tending the little store across the street from where they lived for years as far as he could remember. What kind of life would he give her? And he was Muslim too! The sacrifices she would have to make. Kajol his sister, the girl in the tight jeans and tops, the girl who spoke her mind; where would she be? And then it struck him! Where would Eva be if she had married him? A middle class, sari clad housewife who would be expected to wait upon her in-laws; an outcast who didn't speak a word of Bengali; who would look as out of place at traditional and religious ceremonies and gatherings as a She wouldn't be Eva any more. She would be some stranger that his family would turn her into; she wouldn't even know herself anymore. He pictured her at saraswati puja; lost with not a clue in the world as to what to do next, what was acceptable and what was not, what was expected of her and what wasn't, what would mean crossing the boundaries of decency and acceptance. And to crown it all, just as he had thought of Arif as Muslim, Eva was catholic – or at least he thought she was. Damn it! He didn't even know what God she worshipped and if at all she did; and he had proposed marriage and was mentally making all those plans. And he had felt cheated and dejected and let down by her. But had he been fair to expect her to go along with what he wanted? Had he thought of how she would fit in just as he had thought how Kajol would do as Arif's wife? Eva was Spanish for God's sake; what could she possibly want with a middle class Bengali household and a traditional mother in law. Suddenly it all seemed to make sense to Ari. The pain he had felt was less strong than when Eva had told him she wasn't ready for marriage. What a weird world this was. Life was a major mess up. Nothing made sense anymore. Nothing seemed to matter. It was over; Kajol had made her choice just as Eva had. And if he had respected one woman, then he must respect the other. What did it matter that one was his little sister and the other, the woman who had turned him down. What did it matter that one was Bengali and the other Spanish? They were both women after all. He didn't care what his family thought anymore. She was woman and she had gone after what she wanted. Eva was woman too. Somewhere deep down he felt strangely happy that she had taken control of her life and done what he lacked the courage to do. He didn't feel the pain of loss anymore. It was time to let go...and begin again.

THE CITY OF JOY

A story of survival, love and honour set in the slums of urban India; a story that crosses the boundaries of religion, caste, creed, social status and more; a story of life in the City of Joy.

The silence of the night was broken the rhythmic breathing of 14 year old Farhan, 12 year old Farah and little Afreen. The children lay side by side in the semi darkness; facing each other, their bodies curved almost fetus like. The light from the streetlamp shone into the tiny room and cast gloomy twisted shadows along the wall. The stench of sweat and urine and the heat were unbearable but the children seemed not to be affected by it. Years of endurance had made them immune; it was what they breathed in from the time they came wailing into this world. Afreen lay awake in the darkness taking in the sounds of the room and those outside.

At the far end of the room hung a flimsy curtain that had once been part of a woman's colorful sari, behind which Rihana and Aftaab lay together…arms wound around each other and sweating in the stifling heat. Aftaab shifted in the darkness and groaned and Rihana came to meet him, her body soft, curvaceous and willing. Afreen listened to their sounds as she lay in the darkness and looked towards the curtain. She wondered what the sounds meant, and the movements behind the screen. The child closed her eyes and pressed her head into her brothers back. He heard the sounds grow louder and he thought he knew what the sounds meant but instinct told him it was not something that Afreen should be made wise of at her tender age and so he remained silent and lay listening and turned his attention to the mosquitoes that had begun to sting. The house swarmed with them. They buzzed in the children's ears and stung with a vengeance. They caused sleepless nights, red inflamed bites that itched and wept and got infected due to the lack of hygiene in the poor little souls who knew no better; illiterate as they were.

Farhan was old enough and by all rights should have been in school. He would run each morning to stand outside the big school and watch the big yellow buses full of excited, laughing children drive up to the gates. Then there were the shiny cars that drove up and out got parents who kissed their little boys and girls in their neatly washed and ironed uniforms, shiny black shoes and all. Farhan envied them for their shoes most of all. How he would have loved to own a pair of shoes. He wondered what it felt like to wear shoes. He had never had shoes and the summer heat that shone down with a vengeance burned the underside of his tiny feet. When the last of the children had entered and the bell had rung the gates would swing shut and Farhan would be left standing outside by himself; the outsider, the poor boy who didn't belong in this world of shiny cars, clean clothes that smelled of detergent, polished shoes and colorful books. But Farhan didn't really mind. He was happy enough just to be able to watch the children each morning. In the afternoon he couldn't be there to watch the entire process in reverse order as the gates swung open and the children disappeared into the yellow buses and shiny cars that waited their arrival; he was busy working at the local cycle shop repairing punctures and oiling jammed chains.

He had been sent to work at the shop when he was eight. His parents thought him old enough to earn an income. After all they did have to feed him and the other children and, Aftaab being a daily wage labourer who sat at the crossroad outside Mithai sweet shop waiting for work to come his way, didn't really earn enough to feed his growing family. Aftaab secretly detested them for this and dreaded the day when they would send six year old Afreen out to earn her keep too. He was protective of his little sister and came to her aid whenever she needed him. Why only last week he had clouted Raju, one of the slum hoodlums who thought he could tease Farah. He had chased her home with a stick and called her names. Farah had cried all the way home until Farhan who had been walking home early from the shop where he worked had caught sight of Raju and the object of his teasing and had thrashed him soundly.

Farhan thought of the days when he had managed to earn up to five rupees a day. That was way back then before the likes of Biju and Hari had opened their cycle repair shop across the street from Ali, his owner had his. And before Biju and Hari had bought the big machine that ran on electricity that they illegally consumed from the pole nearby and pumped air into cycle tyres, scooter tyres and even car tyres. Everyone who needed air went to Biju and Hari these days. Only a few loyal cyclists came to Ali's shop with its old hand pump that Farhan used to inflate tyres while they waited on the old wooden stool that Ali provided for them.

Hari and Biju monopolized business with the fancy new air machine, the new red plastic chairs and the glasses of cold water they provided customers. They quite prided themselves on their service and didn't hesitate to let people know that they did a much better job than Ali across the street. Farhan often wondered why Ali didn't think it necessary to improve his service to customers and attract some of them away from Biju and Hari and was given to think that Ali was afraid of the competition until one day Ali asked him to accompany him to the doctor. Almost all of Ali's money went to paying for his daughter Huwaida's treatment. The girl was born with a tumour in her brain and would need surgery soon. Ali knew that he had not the means to pay for it and he also knew that eventually Huwaida would die. Meanwhile he and his wife Fatma who worked as a maid in the big white house that belonged to some businessman not far from the slum where they lived did what they could to keep her alive. It was his duty he said, when he saw the look on Farhan's face. And it was the will of Allah.

Farhan thought about Ali and his daughter long after he got home. He couldn't sleep that night and for many nights after that. He wondered why his parents didn't stop having children; especially since they couldn't afford to feed them. He had seen the mothers and fathers outside the school with only one or sometimes two children. Why did they have to be three? And he knew that the fourth was growing and making its presence felt inside his mother's rounding belly. Farhan felt a sharp pang of guilt; it wasn't his place to be thinking such thoughts. But he couldn't help it. He saw how much his mother slogged each day, how she sweated and worried over how to keep her family fed. And he knew that his father worked hard too; sweated it out painting walls, digging drains, whitewashing buildings and doing any other odd jobs that came his way to make a living. Why then did they make more babies when they could barely feed the ones they had, he wondered. Sometimes as he sat watching his mother stir the cooking pot where rice boiled, he was tempted to broach the subject and ask her why she allowed his father to do the thing that made babies to her; why she gave herself to him so willingly when she had to slog so hard all day. Why did she groan under him from behind the curtain each night he wondered? One day she caught him staring at her as she stirred the rice for the night meal but when he caught her eye, he had not the courage to ask and quietly got up to go for a walk by himself.

Farhan walked down to the wharf at the edge of the slum, the area where the dhobi ghaat was; where colourful sari's were set out to dry and the air was filled with the rhythmic beat of the men beating the cloth upon the stone to get the dirt out from it. The strong scent of bleach and detergent filled the air. It was a clean smell, a smell so different from the one in his home. It was a smell that Farhan liked and he closed his eyes and imagined himself smelling like that, wearing clean clothes and shoes. What would he not have given to own a pair of shoes. Farhan looked down at his dirty calloused feet and sighed. Then he turned and walked towards a group of boys who called to him to come join them for a game of cricket or 'Kirkit' as they called it. Farhan went over and during the course of the game managed to hear that Rizwan, one of the older boys who often bullied them, had been instrumental in forcing his fourteen year old sister into prostitution and that she could be seen every night at the corner of one of the posh streets waiting to be picked up by someone. The boys laughed and cracked lewd jokes at her expense. Farhan thought of Farah and couldn't bring himself to join in their laughter. He told them he had to go home.

On the way home he wondered if Farah would end up the same way. Would she be sent out to sell herself to men for a price? Or would their parents send her out to beg? He'd heard it whispered that his mother was once a whore who entertained an array of men and pleasured them for a price until she had met Aftaab and he had fallen prey to her charms and married her. Some even said she had tricked him into marriage by getting pregnant with the bastard Farhan, and Aftaab being a good man had not dishonoured her and taken her as his wife. The thought of his mother standing at the corner of some dimly lit Street, exposing herself and writhing under the body of some sweaty man behind a flimsy curtain in a hovel of a room in some back alleyway somehow made the bile rise up in his throat and cause his head to throb and he pushed the thought from his mind and walked on. And he wondered what would become of Farah and of little Afreen. The thought of strange men invading her privacy both irked and angered him and he vowed never to let her end up that way. All he had to do was figure out how he was going to prevent that from happening.

By the time he got home it was dark. The frogs and the crickets had set up a constant rhythmic croaking and the sounds of the night took charge of the slum. The cooking fires were lit outside every home and the familiar sight of women bent over the cooking pots that sent an array of smells into the air met Farhan's eyes as he walked home. He passed Ali's home on the way and saw him playing with three year old Huwaida; Huwaida who would soon die for lack of money and medical care. It pained Farhan to think of her in such a manner but that was the reality of her life; it was the reality of every slum dwellers life. He wondered how Ali and Fatma felt each time they looked at her. Ali waved and called to him to come over and share a cup of chai but the thought of the dying girl bothered him and so he politely declined and hurried in the direction of home.

Rihana was dishing out the food into the scooped, earthen plates when he got home. They were celebrating she said. Aftaab had managed to secure a whitewashing contract with a builder that would keep him employed for the next two months at least. It was the new supermarket that was coming up he said. He would be paid sixty rupees a day he said. He had received his first days wages; sixty rupees in all and he had gone out and bought fish for the family to eat. That night they feasted on fish and rice and they even had the luxury of a jalebi each. Farhan knew how much Farah loved jalebis, and even more he was aware of how much of a rarity they were in the household so he hung on to his and wrapped it in a piece of paper and thrust it into his pocket where it would lie until later that night when he and Farah sat on the steps of the abandoned building and listened to an old radio that they had hidden there. Then he would give it to her. It made him happy to see her eyes light up each time he gave her something. And to watch her eat it in relish taking tiny little bites and sucking the sweet sugar syrup out of each little bit before chewing it up as if this would make it last longer always made him smile. He wished he could give her more. And he told himself once again that he had to find a way to give her more.

That night as they sat on the steps and listened to the radio; to the bollywood tunes that filled the air, Farah munched on her jalebi, taking tiny little bites as usual and savouring each bite as if it were a delicacy. Farhan watched her and smiled to himself. She was so innocent and bright eyed. He must not let that be taken away. Her childlike innocence and manner must be untainted. Tomorrow he promised himself he would talk to Ali. Ali was a good man and he would help him find a way to take care of his sister.

It wasn't until lunch time when the two of them sat across from each other and shared Farhan's dry chapattis and Ali's biryani and raita that Farhan dared to broach the subject of Farah. Hesitantly, he poured out his heart to Ali and told him of his fears for his sister's future. Ali listened gravely while Farhan spoke and seemed to pay all his attention to the meal at hand. When he was done, he took a drink of water from a bottle that he kept in the shop, rinsed out his mouth and wiped it on his sleeve. Then he looked at Farhan and spoke. "It is sad that Farah will end up on the streets. There isn't much you or anybody can do to prevent that. However there is a slim chance that we may be able to lie our way into getting the sisters at the convent to take her in. There she will be safe. She will be given food and care, sent to school and taught a trade. When she grows up, she will be given in marriage to some man in search of a wife." Ali stopped and looked at Farhan for a reaction. He told the boy to think it over and went back to work. Farhan joined him and no more was said on the subject.

That night once again, Farhan couldn't sleep. He tossed and turned and thought about what Ali had said. He wondered if it would be right to send Farah to live with the sisters of charity. And what would happen to her there? Would she be happy? Would she miss her mother and cry for her each night? Would they take good care of her? Or would these people send her out to beg as well? Or worse...would they... and Farhan stopped the thought right there. Ali said they were good, kind people. He said they could be trusted. But when Farah grew up she would be married off to some Christian man. And they would teach her their religion. Farhan knew very little of God and religion apart from the fact that Allah was the almighty, the giver and taker of all things. And these people thought different. They would make a non believer of his little sister. Was it a fair price to pay; her safety in exchange for her religion? The thought rankled Farhan all night and for many nights after that. In the days to follow he did not broach the subject again with Ali and Ali in turn did not question him about it. Ali knew it was a hard decision for him to make. And he knew it would take time.

And what would Farah think of being made to leave her home? Would she feel cheated when she knew that her brother had taken her to the sisters not to visit, but to stay? Would she pine for him when he had left? Would she hate him for the rest of her life? And the thought that troubled him the most was how on earth was he to explain to a twelve year old why he was doing this? What did she know of the world? What did she know of prostitution and men and sex? Farhan squeezed the tears that had begun to form out and wiped his eyes before more began to flow. He buried his face in his arms and tried to concentrate on sleep that continued to evade him. In the end he gave in and cried as he lay in the darkness while his family slept all around him.

Farah woke one morning to find Farhan staring at her from the corner of the room where he sat on an old wooden box that served as a stool. The fact that his little sister smiled her most charming smile at him; a smile she reserved only for Farhan who she thought the world of failed to solicit a smile in return bothered her and all at once the smile faded and replaced itself, almost automatically with a look of worry coupled with fear. It was the kind of look that said, "What have I done now?" Farhan walked over to where she lay on the floor and dropped down beside her to put her fears at rest. Rihana was busy with the baby, Afreen who demanded all her attention. And then there was the one that stirred within her and would soon be a child that cried and yelled and demanded to be the centre of Rihana's world and wouldn't settle for any less. That would be about when Afreen would be set aside and slowly forgotten. Just like Farhan had been with the arrival of Farah, and later Farah had been with the arrival of Afreen. It was a vicious cycle; each time a new baby arrived someone lost out but things didn't change. The world went on as before. Farhan hated the fact that Farah had been shelved by their mother and left to fend for herself at such a young age. He hated the baby that moved within her even before it was born and he pitied little Afreen; she would be cast aside too and that was her lot.

That evening when Farhan got home from work he took Farah up to the abandoned building where they sat in silence for a while. Farah sensed the change in her brother's mood and asked him if he was all right. He smiled and said, "Farah, how would you like to go away and live in a nice, clean smelling room with other girls? Would you like to go to school in clean clothes and learn to be somebody important?" Farah looked at him, her eyes shining in the moonlight. She wanted so much to tell Farhan that she would love to go but...the words refused to form themselves on her lips that night. She just sat there in silence. Farhan repeated his question eagerly and shook her by the arm. Only then did he notice the big wet tears that rimmed the dark eyes and flowed down his sister's beautiful face. Only then did he see that she no longer was the child that he had wanted her to be. Only then did he see the woman in her. And he knew; Farah had been inducted into womanhood. She had been robbed of her innocence. The blood rushed to his head and his face flushed, hot with anger. "Who was it?" he asked.

Farah put her arms around him and wept, all the while silencing him and soothing his anger as a mother would a spoiled child. "Who?" he repeated between sobs. Farah buried her head in his shoulder and sobbed. And in between sobs she told him of the time when their mother had been ill and had gone to stay with Kusum, the wife of one of Aftaab's friends who tended to her and how she had been sent to watch her mother when Kusum and her husband Raja had gone to work. She told him of how Raja's brother Mahesh had watched her as she bathed at the communal water tap; of how he had watched her every move, watched her tend to her mother, watched her get dressed after a bath and how when she had least expected it, he had come up behind her and placed his hand on her thigh.

Farhan could take it no more. "Baas!" he cried. His ears seemed on fire and his face bore the contorted, twisted look of a murderer. Blood would be spilled in the slum, of that he was sure. Farah read his mind; she begged him to stop. She didn't want him going to jail she said. She didn't want her child to grow up fatherless she begged.

It was more than Farhan could take. A harami; his own sister's child! He knew he must not let it happen. He remembered the taunts of the other boys. He heard them even after all these years. He thought again of the woman on the street corner, the flimsy curtain in some dimly lit room and of his mother and sister. Their faces flashed before his eyes in turn and seemed to melt into each other.

When Rihana woke in the early hours of the morning, she

tripped over something that lay in her path; something large and heavy that didn't belong there. In the faint moonlight that flitted into the room when she drew aside the curtain she made out the body of Farah. The blood had flowed from her middle onto the rug she lay on and soaked through into the earth beneath. The knife was still embedded in her; the thick blade halfway concealed by the flesh of her body with the blackened handle protruding at a gruesome angle. Her eyes bore the expression of meekness and acceptance as though she almost knew her end had come and accepted it without question or struggle as she was taught to do; as though it were the will of Allah the giver and taker of life.

Somewhere far away, on the other side of the river, Farhan spread out his prayer mat and fell to his knees for the fajr prayer. "Bismillah —a-rehmaan-o-rahim..." he began. Allah was all merciful. He would forgive. As the grey of dawn approached and filled the morning sky, and as the city came to life with the sounds and smells of the early morning vendors and the constant stream of traffic, Farhan let the tears flow. Then he rolled up his mat, dabbed his eyes on the sleeve of his dust covered shirt, puckered his lips as if to suck up the salt from his tears and disappeared into the throng of the City of Joy.

THE KEYS

It was chance, the hand of fate, touch and go. In a city where love has a whole new meaning and happiness is a thing of the past. Where marriage is a piece of paper... everything depends on the Keys.

Wednesday night 8pm. Anjana Mitra looked into her mirror and thought, "Am I beautiful enough?" the look on her face almost expected the mirror to reply to her question. She put on her makeup, brushed out her long wavy hair, colored and styled earlier that day so as to hide the grey streaks that were beginning to make their presence known and finally, when she was satisfied with her appearance, she stood up to dress. Her lingerie was carefully chosen; flimsy bits of lace that revealed a lot of skin; and then the little black dress; the LBD that showed off the curves of her body to the fullest.

It was almost time for Arun, her husband to get home from work. Arun had only just turned forty five, and was CEO of one of the largest firms in the city. The Mitra's lived in a five bedroom Villa that the company had rented for him. Arun drove a BMW but Anjana preferred the more classy Mercedes. She shopped at the most expensive stores and seemed to have no qualms at all about spending her husband's money. Arun too didn't seem to mind. To him Anjana's sometimes indiscriminate spending was a reality that he had learned to live with and one that didn't really make a huge dent in his credit card. On the whole the Mitra's lived a comfortable lifestyle, saw very little of each other, and made sure they were seen together in public often enough and took the annual holiday or so to some exotic island so as to avoid raised eyebrows and unwanted questions from family and friends; traditionalists as they thought of them.

It wasn't that they didn't love each other. Anjana and Arun both cared for each other. They had been married fourteen years now. And in those fourteen years though they had aged and Arun had gotten himself a beer belly and a few grey hairs, he was still a charming man and a very attractive man to look at. Anjana seemed to have weathered the years better than Arun and besides she was a good seven years younger and would soon be thirty eight. But somehow that didn't seem to be enough. The marriage was there, and there didn't seem to be any threat of it ceasing but the magic was all gone. They were down to the mundane... of marriage and everyday living. Except for nights like this when there was always the possibility of the keys changing things even if only for a few fleeting moments.

Alistair D'Cruz walked in to find his wife in her bath. He threw his briefcase on the ottoman in the bedroom upstairs, took off his tie and shoes, walked over to the tiny bedroom bar and poured himself a drink. When he had let the fluid burn its way down his throat he undressed and got in the bath with Payal, who was the most beautiful woman he had ever seen; the woman who stole his heart away seven years ago. This was the woman he had married much against his family's wishes. The search for a 'Goan, catholic girl' had intensified when Alistair was twenty nine and it was then that the two had gone to court and married. A year later they had both moved to the middle-east when Payal, a property lawyer, had got a job with a law firm. Alistair had not been so lucky and it was about five months later that he had managed to find employment in the large automobile industry. The job was good and he had been with the company ever since. Six years later, he lived a comfortable life, enjoyed the privilege of a good home and a fancy car, not to mention the attractive salary package that came with it all.

They were both successful people and enjoyed their challenging careers. They had, over the years become creatures of habit. They dined together each night except on weekends like this when they enjoyed the company of friends and one of the many five star hotels in town. Other than dinner together and an hour or so of TV together before going to bed, where depending on the mood there would or wouldn't be great sex, the couple saw little of each other and had no time to even consider starting a family. Payal didn't seem to want children; her figure would be ruined she said. Alistair made no complaints and so life went on as usual for the D'Cruz's.

They lay in the bath touching and kissing and ended up having great sex. As he made love to her, Alistair wondered if he would be as lucky later that night...or would he have to wait to hold his wife again. He pushed the thought from his mind, as though unwilling to admit to himself the fact that the thought rankled him, stepped out of the bath and began to towel himself dry. Payal followed, took a sip of her husband's whisky and went into the bedroom to get dressed.

She selected a sexy midnight blue mini dress that showed a lot of cleavage with matching heels and clutch. As Alistair looked at her standing there, something deep inside of him didn't want to go. He wished they could get undressed and spend the night at home. They could have he thought, if it weren't for the keys.

The lobby of the Intercontinental hotel was as usual filled with people, chatting, laughing and on their way to one of the many restaurants, pubs or bars. At the far end, mounted on a platform was a mini grand that somebody was playing. The attendants stood stiffly in uniform, ready to assist. The chandelier that hung low from the ceiling cast shadows on the floor below and glittered in the subdued lighting. The scent of 'bakhoor' hung thickly in the air. Upstairs, from the pub 'Al Ghazal, a European group performed live; music from the eighties to the present day stuff and the strains of which could be heard as one stepped out of one's car to enter the lobby. On the first floor at the far end of the balcony was the John Barry bar room, frequented by the upper strata of society. The rich and famous of the city gathered there on weekends for varied purposes. Some did it out of boredom; for lack of anything else to do. Others did it simply for the pleasure of soaking in the laid back ambience; the big heavy couches scattered in little groups all across the room, the dim lighting, the soft music and the sexy voice of the female crooner. And then there were some, who gathered to meet friends, to show off their women like possessions out on display in the market place; as though waiting for a bid for them while still others were there simply for the purpose of being there.

Alistair and Payal walked into the bar and took their usual place in the far corner of the room where the lighting was particularly soft, the music not to loud and the view around them was perfect. They were approached by a waitress in a short skirt that showed off her legs to the advantage of the males around who watched her with appreciative glances. "The usual for me" Payal told the waitress who smiled and nodded. She knew from past experience that Payal wasn't an experimental drinker and preferred to stick to her usual white rum. Alistair, on the other hand, couldn't seem to figure out which scotch he preferred; Blue label or Glenfidditch. He alternated from one to the other, depending on the mood he was in. They were served a few minutes later and the waitress placed before them a bowl of pistachios, almonds and roasted cashews. "Enjoy you drink" she said in her most artificially genuine voice followed by the briefest of smiles and was gone to take the next order and repeat the same for the guests at the table once again.

Back at the bar Alicia, the waitress who had served them looked at the couple seated at the far end of the room, sipping their drinks in silence, barely looking at each other. She thought about her own life and her own husband back home who was, at this very moment putting the kids to bed while she did the night shift at the bar. She was grateful for the fact that they communicated a lot better than the two people she had just served. She made a mental note to tell her husband Mike how thankful she was to have him.

Arun drove in silence. Anjana seated beside him, listened to the songs that. 90.4 FM played. They preferred not to talk. There would be enough talking later. Arun hated the channel but kept it going and put up with it for the fifteen minute drive just to keep Anjana from nagging at him for not letting her listen to her favourite songs. He'd rather plug in his ipod. As they drove into the parking lot, Anjana smoothened out her dress, checked her makeup and adjusted her bra so as to ensure that her ample bosom could be best viewed. She knew there would be appreciative eyes tonight. But it all depended on the keys. Arun watched her and didn't seem to mind at all that his wife was setting herself up for display. They were past that stage now. This was the reality of their lives; a reality that they accepted without question.

At the table with Payal and Alistair, they were joined by Faizal Haque and his new wife from Uzbekistan, Jameela. Faizal was Alistair's ex boss and his wife Jameela had been part of the team that he had worked with; that was until, despite the fact that she spoke very little English and did almost no work except make numerous trips to Faizal's cabin and be available whenever he called, Jameela was promoted to Head of marketing and he, Alistair, who had worked so hard and was counting on the promotion was passed over, he decided to quit altogether. Rumour had it that she had got the position by taking special care of the boss; a rumour that nobody in the office seemed to doubt.

It wasn't until Alistair had climbed the ladder of success and reached a top level managerial position that they had seemed to run into each other in the same social circles. And Jameela's trips to his cabin had paid off. She was the new Mrs. Haque and the fact that she was twenty six and he was fifty two didn't seem to matter at all. Jameela, dressed in her usual mini skirt that revealed her ample long legs, the halter burgundy top that contrasted sharply with her milky white skin and the look of hunger in her eyes wasn't lost on any of the others. As for who would get lucky tonight; everything depended on the keys.

They six people seemed to form an elite little group. They were the regulars there. They knew almost everybody and everybody knew them; but only on the surface. They saw only the side that they chose to let everyone see. They drank and laughed and throughout their drinking, the eyes of Faizal and Arun wandered to the women other than their own wives; they admired their bodies openly and shamelessly and lusted after them with their eyes. Alistair looked, but was ill at ease. He wasn't as seasoned as the others when it came to the matter of the keys.

The keys, the deciding factor once again. Aliatair's chain of thought was broken with the arrival of Nandini and Charles Menezes and Maya and Devinder Khurana, also part of this little group of regulars at the bar and who gathered there with the common purpose in mind. The men looked around them scrutinizing the two women that now sat before them. Maya in her late thirties; dark skinned but beautiful, and Nandini; fair and pretty; with a body that would put a model to shame. Almost at once the men were making mental calculations and lusting after her at the same time.

The waitress materialized once again, took orders and disappeared. Once they had been served conversation flowed somewhat freely as the women discussed the newest places to shop in town and the men discussed the usual; fishing, golf, business and money. The most carefully avoided topic of the night was relationships. However, they flirted blatantly with each other's spouses; Jameela had her hand on Alistair's thigh. It was clear she fancied him for his youth and good looks. Anjana seemed to have a lot in common with Faizal Haque and discussed the art exhibition at the centre for Culture and Learning. Arun vied with Devender for Nandini's attentions and couldn't seem to take his eyes of her.

As the night wore on and the scotch and wine flowed more freely, the people seated around the table began to loosen up and their laughter got louder and the jokes got lewder. When they had seemingly run out of things to say to each other and a heavy awkward silence made its presence known, Nandini opened her handbag and produced dark green a silk pouch which she placed on the table before them. The animated banter ceased almost immediately and they waited with bated breath. One by one the men placed in it their car keys; only the single keys, the rings removed and passed it around. Then it was ruffled up, and set aside. Faizal took a piece of paper, tore it into five pieces and scribbled a number from 1 to 5 on each. He folded the pieces meticulously, cupped his palms together, shook them around and threw them on the table. Each woman there reached out to pick up one. Payal picked one so she would get first pick at the keys in the bag. Nandini drew number two and would be second. Anjana, who drew five would have to settle for leftovers tonight; not something she was happy about. But then on second thought what difference did it make. Everything depended on chance...everything depended on the keys.

Payal put her hand into the bag and withdrew it quickly. The rules were there was to be no feeling around inside the bag for familiar keys. It had to be one single quick thrust into the bag and out. The key she held in her hand, by some miracle of chance was that of her husband's Jaguar; a fact she accepted with resignation. She loved her husband, but she also had a taste for wild lovemaking and the fact that she enjoyed her times with Faizal, were common knowledge in the little group. She had chosen her husband...or was it chance that they had been brought together this time. That left four women and four men in the group. Jameela clearly did nothing to hide the fact that she was disappointed; the thought of having Alistair make love to her had aroused her. Nandini chose and it was Devender's key that she held in her hand. Anjana came up with Charles key in turn and Jameela with Arun's key. Maya would be going home with Faizal tonight. It was decided. The keys had decided. It was time to go. Each of the women picked up their bags and left with the man whose car key they had chosen. They gave their own spouses the perfunctory goodbye and the "see you tomorrow" and were gone. It was a simple as that. There was no time for second thoughts or regret. There would be no turning back now; no opportunity to rewind and go back to the time before they had each reached into the little silk pouch and discover what the night had to offer up to them.

On the drive back to their luxury apartment in one of the more upper class parts of the city, Alistair and Payal both seemed relieved to be together. Things could have been a lot worse. Payal didn't particularly care for Devender Khurana and spending an entire night in his bed was something she wasn't exactly looking forward to. Faizal Haque was an exciting lover; one that believed in pleasuring his woman. But when she was with Alistair it was different. It was what she had had grown accustomed to. It was what she loved.

For the others, the decision of the keys was binding for that night. The women had their pick and the men took what they got and went home and made the best of it. They were supposed to be friends, these men and so they found no wrong in a little wife swapping once in a while. They needed change they said in justification. The wives seemed not to care. They enjoyed secure marriages; they knew the men they had married were suckers and would not leave them for one reason another; the children, the family and its honor, the parents, and society in general. But mostly because it was convenient for them to be married to these women who complacently accepted this part of their lives as 'much needed change.' And they secretly enjoyed it too. These were women who cared little for traditional marriage values though they argued that they did; that was why their marriages were intact in the first place. These were women who needed more than what their spouses gave them in the way of sex, and they were not ashamed to get their satisfaction at all cost.

A month later, Anjana took the flight back after almost a month with her in-laws; a month of being a dutiful, traditional wife and an exceptional daughter-in-law. Arun's parents were so proud of her. She shuddered at the memory. But she was back now, and as she drove home in the back seat of a taxi; Arun had phoned to say he was in a meeting and couldn't pick her up, she thought about what she would wear later that night. As she did a rush of adrenalin shot through her entire being and seemed to bring her to life. It was Wednesday night and once again, the keys would decide.

THE CONFESSION

"Father forgive me for I have sinned...in thought, in word and deed; in what I have done and in what I have failed to do..." It was as easy as that...or was it? Only the clergyman knew.

Priya Shankaran sat in church, head slightly cocked to one side, a wisp of thick dark hair that had somehow gotten loose partly covered the side of her face and listened intently to the Reverend McGill's Sunday morning sermon. She liked hearing the sound of his deep throaty voice; as if it were that of God himself. She liked the way he seemed to roll his 'R's'. It sent a warm feeling of being alive down her body and into her toes. This morning's sermon was better than good. It was thought provoking and touched a nerve somewhere in her being to say the very least. She had sought out the time to come to church and she knew she would not be disappointed. She was a tall, dark skinned attractive woman with curves in all the right places. She focused on the Reverend and as her gaze met his fleetingly, he coughed and reached for his glass of water.

The Reverend Richard McGill got up from his morning prayers and prepared to face the day. He was a man of habit and rose at precisely 5am, washed and dressed and then knelt to spend time in communion with the Lord as he often put it after which he read his Bible and spent time in reflecting on the word. On weekdays he breakfasted at 7:00am, a task that took him no more than twenty minutes after which, clad in pyjamas and dressing gown he climbed the stairs to his first floor bedroom and prepared to get dressed for the day.

When he had donned his cassock and girdle, he picked up his well used, dog-eared, Bible and placed it in his brown leather custom made briefcase. Then briefcase in hand he walked the short distance from his parsonage to the Church office where he spent the entire morning at work buried in a pile of papers replying to correspondence, updating records, attending meetings and the like until one o clock, when he walked back to the parsonage for lunch and his hour of reading followed by an afternoon siesta. At 4pm he was served coffee by his housekeeper cum cook Martha, who knew just how he liked his coffee brewed and never got it wrong. When the big mug of steaming black coffee had been downed, Reverend McGill began his evening rounds of visiting the sick of his parish, administering the sacraments to those who needed it, celebrating a birth or a baptism or funeral, and generally attending to the spiritual needs of his parishioners. The spiritual care of his flock was the primary concern of Reverend McGill. He prided himself on the fact that he knew every family quite well; he knew where they lived and worked or if they didn't work, how many children they had, and visited regularly enough to familiarize himself with them and make himself approachable when it came to telling him their problems. They always found a listener in Reverend McGill, who never failed to give them sound advice. His parishioners looked up to him as their father, friend, brother and mentor. On the whole, he was well liked and respected in the little parish that was his.

Reverend McGill had come to the parish almost fifteen years ago, a young lad of twenty three as an assistant to the old priest who was then in charge of the church. Old Reverend Kenneth Ashton, a veteran of seventy six was retiring in a year's time and Reverend McGill had been sent by the Bishop to take charge from him. He had learned well and had done a good job with his parish. He had focused on the spiritual coming together of his flock each Sunday and his sermons were short and sweet but truly enriching. His parishioners came to church not just out of a sense of duty, but out of a thirst for the word of the Lord that Reverend McGill managed to put across to them in a manner that appealed to young and old alike. No one yawned in Reverend McGill's church. Worship was a time to be alive and filled with the spirit of good.

Reverend McGill had never married. He had once been engaged to the daughter of the bank manager but nothing had come of it and the relationship had fizzled out. Then there had been talk of his 'involvement' with another woman but it hadn't materialized either. Some said that at thirty eight, Reverend McGill was a confirmed bachelor who had devoted his life to the service of God and humanity while others thought that he simply hadn't found a woman who was worthy of being a Reverend's wife and living up to the title.

On Sunday's the Reverend followed a different schedule. He walked into church at precisely 7:15 am and prepared for the eight o clock service. He ensured the holy sacrament was ready, the Bible opened to the page from where the reading would be done, the flowers in the vases were arranged, the candles lit and other such matters that needed taking care of. Then in a freshly laundered cassock and vestments, the Reverend celebrated the service for that morning.

When service was over he stood at the entrance to the church and greeted each of his parishioners as they walked out into the churchyard to enjoy a cup of fellowship tea and cakes. He would disappear into his vestry for a minute or two, to change out of his vestments and clad in his Sunday morning suit he would spend time in fellowship with the faithful. The ladies never failed to come over to chat about something or the other; one wanted to know if she should go ahead and put up the streamers for the Easter festivities in the yard, another wanted more ribbon, another showed off the new altar cloth she had hand embroidered and so on. They all vied for his attention shamelessly and seemed to forget, for the moment that he was the Reverend. Their husbands stood close at hand and smoked while their women folk devoted their attentions to the Reverend. They took no offense for they saw in him no formidable opponent. Their women were safe.

Priya Shankaran was an admirable young mother of two boys aged seven and five. She was a schoolteacher at the local school and was married to Shankaran Krishnamurthy, a well to do businessman who wasn't too happy with her and their life together because she had chosen Christ as her personal saviour and had been baptised of her own free will. Priya no longer adhered to the custom of performing the morning ritual of 'pooja' in the Krishnamurthy home. Her best friend and colleague, Katrina Krum had been instrumental in her growing in knowledge of the Lord in a significant way. Priya had responded positively and her apparent love for the Lord had resulted in her baptism. Shankaran resented his wife's association with the church and his son's initiation to Christianity. He saw it as a personal vendetta against him and the peacefulness and sanctity of his home.

Priya worked hard at her job and was good at it. Her dedication was appreciated by her superiors and she took pride in the fact that she was a good worker. Her children were as children should be; happy and content for the most part though the older boy at seven, was beginning to feel the depth of the void created when his father had stopped spending time with him, the excuse being he was too tied down with work. He wanted someone to play baseball with him, he wanted someone to take him fishing, he wanted someone to help him make paper boats and to float them in the puddles in the backyard after the rain. He also wanted someone to be there when he was in the school concert and to clap and cheer him on like the other parents did. Shankaran never did any of those things; not anymore.

She felt her sons need and did her best to make up for a father who chose to remain a stranger to his sons, only because he would not accept the religious beliefs of their mother. The boys were both Hindu; she told them what she knew of Christianity but never once forced upon them her beliefs. Priya tried to make him see reason but she knew she was playing a losing game. She was woman after all; she thought and acted like a woman and fishing and baseball were beyond her league.

Reverend McGill visited Priya whenever he happened to be in the vicinity. He understood the challenges she faced with an unbeliever for a husband and the ridicule that came with it. He understood when she wasn't in Church with her boys on a Sunday and assured her that God was an understanding God and would not hold it against her. Priya appreciated his assurances and was grateful for the Reverend's support. She felt comforted. She knew that God would forgive as he always did, but she needed to hear Reverend McGill say those words to make her feel better.

Priya hadn't been to church for three Sundays in succession. It was unusual for her to miss three Sundays. Perhaps she was out of town; Reverend McGill consoled himself with this thought. Or perhaps her husband had objected to her coming after all. He could do no more than pray for her. And pray he did. But she also filled his thoughts as he went about his routine living. As the days passed he found himself preoccupied with thoughts of what she was doing filling his head more often than was necessary. He thought about the way her dress swished about her knees as she walked, about the sway of her hips and the dark skin of her face and neck, the black hair and dark eyes than seemed to light up at the slightest provocation. The fact that all these details passed so frequently and unashamedly through his mind seemed to bother Reverend McGill. After all, the woman that occupied his thoughts was very married and it was sinful to be thinking of her so unabashedly. He would visit her the coming weekend if she wasn't in church he thought. A regular 'out-of-concern' visit just to check if all was well he thought. He wondered to himself if it were the sensible thing to do. But then she was a parishioner and as parish priest it was his duty to check on all his parishioners he argued to himself. Reverend McGill was no fool and the fact that he needed to justify to his conscience a visit to Priya's home seemed to rankle him. He decided to wait till Sunday and then decide what to do.

Sunday morning worship began at precisely eight. The little church with its small parish of about one hundred and forty people, children included, was filled to capacity. In the third row sat Priya, head bowed and in prayer. Reverend McGill began with a call to worship followed by the opening hymn. It was then that he noticed; she looked thinner, more tired and bore the look of long term suffering that had finally caught up with her.

She sat across him on a couch in his living room. She had wanted to talk she said. And so he had walked her back to his parsonage; more private than his office with its wooden partitions and the secretary and the accounts person paying careful attention to every word that was being exchanged; words that would be carefully distorted and let loose, for the hungry congregation to feed on and sit in judgement over her. The way she crossed her legs disturbed the Reverend; made him lose focus of what she was saying. "I don't love my husband anymore; I can't live with him. I want a divorce" she seemed to be saying. Reverend McGill listened in silence. He knew he should encourage her to pray, to talk it over with her husband, to find the reason of her feeling so, to see a marriage counsellor; he knew it was what she expected him to say. He was Reverend after all and it was he who guided lost sheep and gave them hope when they had lost all of their own. But something deep within the Reverend stirred and manifest itself in his loins. He knew he was sinning but he couldn't stop himself. The very thought was sinful in itself and he mentally muttered a confession. "Father, forgive me for I have sinned" he said guiltily. But that was only the beginning.

That he was committing adultery as he undressed her and made passionate love to her didn't seem to matter anymore. That he would be answerable to God for his deeds was a faraway thought at the moment. That he was begging her to stay with him forever as she cried out for him to make love to her again was the only thing that mattered; the only thing that was real at that moment. She was real; her touch was real. Her body the colour of dark chocolate, like silk beneath his more deeply tanned, was real. And that was all he needed now. The years of living alone had taken their toll on him. He was man, he was human and he lusted after this woman who so willingly gave herself to him. Tomorrow was far away and Sunday was even further...a distant eventuality that he would have to face.

They made love every day after that. She spent the afternoons with him. When Sunday came Reverend McGill dressed himself, vestments and all and stood before his congregation of more than a hundred people and preached on the Ten commandments including "Thou shalt not commit adultery"; he choked on the words and reached for his glass of water. Priya sat through the sermon straight faced and guiltless. She skipped communion and when Reverend McGill looked up from putting away the sacraments, she was gone.

When he climbed the stairs to his bedroom after the last of his parishioners had left, she was waiting for him. Beside the door to his bedroom were a travel case and a matching travel bag. She was here to stay. Priya Shankaran had opted out of her marriage. She had almost gone back on her decision when her husband refused to let her take the boys. Somewhere deep down she had known he wouldn't. And that had made her think about staying. But, in the end, she had decided that she could no longer bear to live with a man so loathsome, who would mark her and leave her scarred. Her body had taken enough. He had followed her the last time she was at the Reverend's home and had ranted and raved about the immorality that her new found faith encouraged; he had cursed the Reverend for defiling his woman. And then he had turned on her with a vengeance like never before. She had had no choice.

Reverend McGill looked at the luggage and sat down heavily upon the edge of the bed. She stood at the window with her back to him. "You shouldn't have come", he said. "It was only when she turned to face him did he see the bruises on her face and he regretted immediately the words that had passed his lips seconds before. She came to him hoping for a hug but he just stood there and stared at her. Finally it was she who broke the silence. "Aren't you going to even ask what happened?" she questioned. Without waiting for an answer she burst into tears. "Don't send me back there. Please! I beg you. I can't live with him any longer." Priya flung her arms around Reverend McGill but he pushed her away. The hurt she felt and not being wanted was evident on her face.

Ten months later, Richard McGill sat in an arm chair in the lobby of a city hotel. He wore beige corduroy trousers, an open necked shirt and a pair of loafers. His hair, only just beginning to grey at the edges, fell lazily across his face. Minus the vestments, the padre's collar and the girdle that looked like it belonged in the middle ages, he looked quite ordinary; definitely more human and quite like any of the other man in the half filled lobby. He was fit, tall and hand-some. He sipped an iced tea and looked around casually. His gaze travelled to the woman in a white maternity dress who was walking across towards him. The baby bump she carried was only just beginning to show. She smiled, and slipped into the chair beside him. As if out of nowhere, the maitre' D materialized. "Good evening Mrs. McGill. Will you be ready to order now?" "Yes" they answered in unison. Dinner was a scrumptious affair. Priya McGill ate heartily; after all she was eating for two.

THE OLD HOUSE

I remember, I remember the old house as it were

With garden overgrown and leaves wind blown

All strewed upon the earthy floor

The silence in the yard I hear

As in through the darkened panes I peered

The old house, the old house the place that I call home

The old house came into sight as soon as we rounded the bend. We had just passed the home of the parish priest; a relatively large old bungalow that looked as if it had seen better days. The high wall and the large gates added to the dismal look of the place. From the little that was visible as we passed the open gate, I saw that the windows and doors were all painted a dark brown; a colour that not only darkened the place but added to the gloominess of the place and chilled me to the bone. I shuddered to think of what came next. I didn't have to wait long. Seconds later, there it was, the old place that was to be our home for a long time to come; certainly longer than any other place I had called home.

At first sight I thought my father must be mistaken. This couldn't be where we were to live. It certainly didn't look like a house to me. The yard was overgrown with knee high grass and in the centre of the front yard with a red brick wall around the place was a well with a hand pump for water. A few feet behind the well stood the house, if at all it could be called that. Dark yellow walls and dirty brown doors and windows with no glass panes in places, replaced with brown paper or even worse newspaper. The tiled roof was missing a few tiles here and there. It was more a shack than a house. And this is what was to be our new home. It was, to say the very least, nothing like our present home; a third floor large three bedroom apartment that we were very comfortable in. We had big French windows in the living room and one of the bedrooms. The other two; the master bedroom and my bedroom had two big windows on either side of a spacious built in wardrobe. In all we were comfortable and loved it. Moving wasn't exactly a welcome idea, especially not to this place.

I had hardly gotten over my shock at seeing the exterior of the house when I was led inside by my father and given a tour of the place. Two rooms and a narrow veranda, not five feet in width, that ran the length of the living room. Off the main square room, was a kitchen and a toilet; the kitchen with two out of four walls being only half built up and from about my waist up, when I stood against it, there was fixed expanded metal that let all the air, dust the tamarind leaves and anything else that chanced to be around from the tree out back into the place and into whatever was cooking if by chance it happened to be left uncovered. I saw no sign of any sink in which to wash dishes and neither was there a tap in sight. When I commented on this fact dad stepped out the back door and showed me a tap about one foot off the ground where water flowed for about two hours each morning and two hours each evening. And it was usually no more than a trickle. So we did have water after all. That was some consolation. The bathroom scenario was not much different. A portion had been set aside for bathing and was surrounded by a little wall about 6 inches off the ground. The rest of the place was almost beyond description; I shall refrain from doing so for the very thought of it makes my skin crawl. However it is worth mentioning that while in the middle of my first bath there I nearly jumped out of my skin and was almost sent running into the living room and the common bedroom that I shared with my grandmother and two grand aunts, in nothing but my birthday suit when a huge toad, disturbed by the splashes of hot water, decided to hop out at me. I especially dislike toads and anything that wriggles; worms, caterpillars and the like are not exactly my thing though I do have a certain fixation with snakes, as long as they choose not to bite that is. I like them from far though I have been in close proximity with them and have not been particularly afraid.

It was the month of February 1997, and I was in my finishing year of school. I was taking the school leaving exams the following month and when we moved into the house of horrors, as I thought of it, I was on study leave which I used to help my father move our stuff in there. The more stuff we brought over the more real was the fact that this is where we were actually going to be living. Though I hated the thought of giving up my own room with its comforts I knew that my father worked hard to take care of us; his mother, two aunts and me. And so it was that we moved into the old house with all its drawbacks.

I graduated from high school that summer of 1997 and it was a memorable summer in more respects than one. We discovered the true meaning of the word 'hot'. The bedroom of the house was a later construction; an extension of the original structure and the people who lived there before us, an old couple, had placed on the roof sheets of asbestos. The walls on two sides of the room were partly brick; up to about four feet in height and the rest was again asbestos sheeting. We boiled and sweated in there all throughout the long summer days but fared better at nights when the sheets cooled off. There was no such thing as air conditioning and a ceiling fan that gave off hot air was the only respite we had.

I slept on what was two single beds joined together so as to accommodate three; my grandmother, one grand aunt and me. Since I was the youngest, I was given no choice but to sleep in between the two women; a position I wasn't exactly too happy about. Having your grandmother snore right into your ears isn't exactly my idea of a restful night's sleep and having the bed creak and shift each time she turned over in her sleep makes me wonder why I ever imagined sleep was good at all. My grandmother, age and its many ailments having caught up with her, walked with some difficulty and the weight of her body was, if I might add, too much for her short little legs to bear. Each time she heaved herself slowly and painfully off the bed, she used some part of my poor unfortunate body for support. Complaining wouldn't have gotten me anywhere as the house wasn't made for so many people and was as full as it could possibly be with no room to spare, or so I thought.

Not long after we had been in the house, dad being the handyman that he was, got down to sandpapering all the years and years of dark brown paint off the doors and windows; if they could be called doors and window frames. I joined in and soon we had everything painted white. We scraped the deep yellow colour cheap distemper off the walls and got down to giving them a few coats of white. I painted the lower half of the walls white in the veranda and later dad extended it to run along the entire length of the house. With time we got a new kitchen sink, a new bathroom floor and managed to block the hole that the frogs and toads used as entrance to our bathroom.

The monsoon set in with a vengeance and though thankful for respite from the excessive heat, we soon realized we had a whole new problem on our hands; a leaky roof! It leaked in places all over the house; about seven places in the living room, including right over the TV, on one of the couches which of course we moved and a number of other corners and wherever a tile had gotten loose or there happened to be a tiny hole in the asbestos sheets that was over our bedroom roof. It even leaked right over our bed! We had to move the bed over a bit and place red plastic basin on the floor to collect the water that dripped in when it rained. All over the house there were buckets, basins, bowls and anything large enough to collect dripping rain water. The house of horrors was living up to its name.

There is nothing so wonderful as an Indian monsoon, so refreshing are the light afternoon showers that give respite from the scorching heat. Everything is green again, there is life and colour and the smell of wet earth mingled with the scent of flowers that fills the air. But when you are out in the street going about your business and you look up to see dark clouds fill the sky beckoning the onset of a thunder shower you quickly rush home to save yourself from being drenched only to find that you have a leaky roof that makes you wet anyway to contend with; now that isn't a very pleasant thought. I particularly dislike the monsoon and despite the fact that my Indian friends seem to think it 'perfectly romantic' weather, I beg to disagree and hold fast to my claim that the monsoon is a dull, dreary season of wet, wet and more wet. Eventually it gets to be quite tiresome and leaves everything damp to the touch and rather smelly.

If I thought that things couldn't possibly get worse, I was sadly mistaken. The yard outside the house was over grown with grass which though we had chopped and burned during the summer, grew right back again the moment the rains set in and housed, in its midst a number of frogs, toads, centipedes, earthworms and other creepy crawlies all of whom I happen to detest. The worst of the lot were the piles of what must have been hundreds of red worms, about an inch long that multiplied at the rate of knots and lay in ever moving piles all around the place. My grandaunt I remember often burned them with hot water for my sake; I refused to step out of the house and shuddered at the very thought of them. I wasn't really afraid. They just gave me the creeps!

And throughout the wet season I refrained from stepping out unless I absolutely had to; I went to no weddings, attended no parties and visited no friends. All I did was go to work because I simply had no choice in the matter.

When the wet was finally over and the damp corners in the house began to dry out and there was sun again I was happier. Autumn arrived and brought with it the falling leaves turned brown and gold and this was the time I was happiest. Autumn brought to me a certain unexplainable joy and warmth that seemed to begin somewhere within the very core of my being. I watched from the doorway the old tree across the field, its spreading branches filled with yellow blossom and suddenly the repulsion that I had felt at living in the old house was lost. It was all gone. All that remained in its place was a feeling of contentment, of belonging and of absolute peace. I remember the fallen autumn leaves, burnt crisp by the sun that crunched under my feet as I walked. The sudden early morning nip in the weather as I sat and sipped a mug of early morning steaming hot tea on the doorstep. The sunshine that flitted in through the open door and filled the house; the white window frames with their painted white grills.

I love Autumn. There is something about the beginning of the cold, the clear azure expanse with fluffy white balls of cotton sailing around, flowers of very hue and the floral scent that fills the air and tickles one's nostrils; the children playing and stretching cramped muscles after being shut inside during the wet season. The field was filled with life and laughter. Our world seemed to have come alive. The birds perched themselves on the tiled roof and sang their song to all those who cared to hear. I did. And it was music to the ears. And the old house of horrors didn't seem so bad anymore.

When winter came, the old house kept us warm enough, close and sheltered from the harsh temperature outside. We had, by now, the beginnings of a garden with potted plants that lined the outside of the living room in a row. The kitchen wall was built up too and so the cold wind didn't get to us. It was filled with warmth; warmth that seeped out from the very walls and filled the place; warmth that we began to feel in our very being, warmth that made us whole. And it was then I realized that the old house of horrors was no longer just that, a house of horrors. It had taken on a whole new existence for me. Suddenly the fact that it was old and dilapidated, the walls cracked, the paint peeling, the doors rickety, the roof leaky, the flooring uneven Kadappa stone didn't seem to matter anymore. The old house was home. It was woven into the many facets of my life and it made me who I am. Years of living in the little old house allowed me to gather and treasure some of the memories we made together back when life was simple and I was home.

In the summer of 2001 our extended family including aunts, uncles, cousins and even a grand aunt and I went on an overnight picnic and had the misfortune of experiencing an earthquake that left its trail of damage in the city. The guest house we had booked into suffered heavily cracked walls; lost more than a few of its roof tiles that fell to the floor with loud crashes and left us trembling in fear. I remember us rushing home at the earliest to ensure that the rest of our families, our homes and our friends were safe. As I rounded the bend in the road just before I caught sight of home I remember feeling tightness in my chest; a feeling I now realize was fear. A few seconds later the sight of my father watering the garden brought an immense sense of relief. The house was still standing in the background; we had lost one tile from the living room roof and had a minor crack in one of the walls. Apart from that, nothing else seemed wrong.

Over the years we shared real good times in our old home. Because we had a yard out front and a big field beyond, the centre of which stood the old church, our home came to be the gathering place for our extended family. Cousins, uncles, aunts, grand aunts, grandparents and friends continued to frequent it and spend many an hour sitting out in the sunshine watching the kids at play. The house of horrors wasn't so bad after all. It sure had its moments.

Late in 2012 when we had begun preparing for Christmas my father took ill and passed away. As he was laid out in the house, loads of friends, family and well wishers came to pay their last respects. After the funeral as I sat looking at the house sharing a cup of coffee with my fiancée I remembered the times when we had just moved in and the hard work and determination of the man who had been my father to get the place to its present state. I wondered what would happen to the house now; would it go back to rack and ruin? I guessed so for there was no one so hard working as dad, no one with the kind of enthusiasm and ideas that he had. And I guess the old house is no longer home.

THE END

www.ingramcontent.com/pod-product-compliance
Lightning Source LLC
Chambersburg PA
CBHW070504170726
48291CB00008B/2642